Corrupted in Corpus Christi

The House Sitters Cozy Mystery Series
Book 0

SCARLETT MOSS

Abby Moss Publishing

Corrupted in Corpus Christi- Scarlett Moss
Copyright © 2019 Scarlett Braden

For information contact :
Scarlett Braden at <u>Scarlett@scarlettbraden.com</u>

This is a work of fiction. Names, characters, places, and incidents either are the product of the author's imagination or are used fictitiously, and any resemblance to actual persons, living or dead, business establishments, events, or locales is entirely coincidental.

ISBN: 9781657351035

Chapter One

"911, what's your emergency please?"

"Hello...May I speak to the sheriff, please? Is he there?"

"Ma'am, this is 911 dispatch. Do you have an emergency?"

"Yes. Yes, I do. But I need to talk to the sheriff. It's rather delicate."

"This line is only for emergency calls. What is your emergency, please?"

"Um...well...um."

"Ma'am, please. If this is not an emergency, please hang up and call the non-emergency number."

"My husband is in the pool."

"I see. And this is an emergency because?"

"He's dead."

"Please stay on the line with me. Help is on the way. What is your name?"

"Marsha."

"What is your address, Marsha?"

"29 Dunwoody Lane"

"Okay, Marsha. Are you in any danger?"

"No, I don't think so."

"Do you know what happened?"

"No, not really. He never came to bed; I came down this morning and he's floating in the pool. He still has his clothes on. You did send the sheriff, right? Not a stranger, I hope! Can you tell him not to turn on his siren? I don't want the neighbors to see. If he could come in his personal car, that would be better."

"Marsha, I'm in the Corpus Christi emergency dispatch office. I'm not sure who is coming to your house. It will be whichever officers were available and closest to your address. But they are coming fast, with sirens, so they can check to see if he's still alive. It might not be too late."

"Oh, he's dead. I know he is."

"How's that? Are you a medical professional?"

"No. I know he's dead because he's been floating like that for an hour."

"An hour? And you just now called 911?"

"I used the pool skimmer to poke him. He didn't move. I thought he was playing a joke on me. I pushed him all over the pool. He didn't move or come up for air once. I realized he still had his clothes on from the party last night. And his shoes. I went inside to get dressed and do my makeup. I was still in my housecoat. Then I called you. I mean he was already dead. How was embarrassing myself going to change anything?"

"I understand. Marsha, what is your husband's name?"

"George."

"What is your last name, Marsha?"

"Oh Lawd, I knew you were going to ask me that. Darn it! Do I have to answer that, or can I plead the fourth? Or third or fifth. Or whatever that is."

"Marsha, do you know the sheriff personally? My name is Joan Arny. Do I know you?"

"Oh, thank goodness! Yes, Joan, of course, this is Marsha Colfax. Can you please send Alen?"

"Dispatch has already sent officers to your location. But I'll get hold of Alen and send him to you as soon as he can get there. I'm so sorry!"

"I hear sirens! Please tell them to turn them off!"

"Okay. Marsha stay on the line with me, I'll tell them to turn them off and I'll be right back."

Joan Arny, wife of Sheriff Alen Arny, motioned to the supervisor on the floor. She requested the approaching officers kill the sirens.

"They are here, I have to open the door for them. You're sending Alen, right?"

"Yes, Marsha. You can hang up now and I'll call Alen."

So much made sense now. And there were so many new questions.

Chapter Two

"Hi, Beautiful! It's not time for your break, yet. What's up?"

"Alen, I just took a call from Marsha Colfax. She called in because...I'm so sorry, but she said George is dead." Joan said, knowing this was a bad way to have to break the news to her husband that his closest friend was dead.

"What? What happened? Was it a heart attack?"

"When she called, she wanted to talk to you. I didn't realize it was her at first. She didn't want a stranger going over there, asked that they turn off the siren, and all that. I didn't understand at first. Anyway, I told her I would send you over if you could go."

"Yes, of course, I'm on my way, but what happened?"

"I don't know. She found him floating in the pool this morning. She said he didn't come to bed. He has his clothes on. They had some kind of party last night. Alen, she waited an hour...while she got dressed and did her makeup, to call 911."

"Well, that does sound like Marsha."

"Alen, I have a bad feeling. Things didn't seem right at all with that call. I asked if she was in danger and she said no, but I wonder..."

"Why, what do you think was wrong? You think someone was there? That she was under duress?"

"Well, no, I don't think so, I mean if a killer was there, they wouldn't let her call 911. Would they?"

"Not usually. Unless..."

"Oh no! Do you think it's a setup? Is that why she asked for you? Don't go!"

"I'm sure it's fine. I'm on my way. The first unit is there, if something is up they'll radio in. If you hear something I need to know, call me, otherwise I'll call you after I get there and let you know what's going on."

"I don't like it, but okay, I understand."

<hr>

George felt like Alen's only family except for Joan. They served together in the Gulf War. While Alen was there, his father died of a heart attack. Three months later, with her son at war and her husband gone, his mother died in her sleep, obviously of loneliness and grief. When it was time to go home, Alen didn't even know where to go. There was absolutely nothing and no one left for him in Phoenix, except for maybe the ex-wife that divorced him six months into his first tour. And he didn't even know if she was still there. Or what her name might be now. Nor did he care. George invited him to go home with him. George and Marsha became his family at that point. Marsha was never a warm and fuzzy sort, but always cordial and welcoming with her Southern grace and hospitality. When it came time for him to retire, Alen came back to

Corpus Christi. To where the only family he had was. He couldn't wrap his mind around George being gone. They were the same age. George had no health problems. Alen couldn't begin to imagine what could have happened to his best friend.

———————◦◦———————

    Alen arrived at the home of his friends Marsha and George Colfax. It was a flat fronted, two-story brick home with a circular drive in front. Across the front of the house on the front porch were five Corinthian white stone columns that always made Alen think of concrete palm trees. Perfectly interspersed between the columns on either side of the front walk to the door in the center of the house were four maturing oak trees the couple kept meticulously trimmed to just below roof level. Across the circular drive was a large manicured and landscape area.

    The ambulance was already there, with the back doors flung open and the gurney missing, apparently already inside. The front door was standing open, as was the privacy fence gate to the right side of the house. Alen opted to go through the gate instead of the house to reach the pool in the back yard.

    Making his way to the back, questions and scenarios were racing through Alen's mind. George was a city councilman; therefore, they entertained a lot. But if they were having a party, Alen and Joan were always invited. Alen's first question was what in the world happened, his second question was why would Marsha go to bed if there was a party going on, and his third question was what kind of party were the Colfaxes having that they were not invited to.

    When he approached the pool area, he identified the officers first on the scene. They were obvious because they were soaking wet from fishing George out of the pool. They were lifting the poor man from the ground onto the gurney. Alen looked around for Marsha. He spotted her on the deck that overlooked the pool with two other officers. Her back was to the pool. The officers would have turned her that way so she wouldn't be traumatized by seeing them maneuver her dead husband out of the pool. That's not ever a graceful task. He nodded at the EMTs and the wet officers on his way to the deck.

Climbing the steps up onto the deck, the first thing Alen noticed, was that Marsha was calm. Well, as calm as anyone in this situation could be. She wasn't hysterical. She wasn't crying. She was perfectly coiffed as usual. Her dark brown hair was in a sleek bob cut, every hair smooth and in place. Her makeup was glamour shot perfect. She was wearing black slacks and a heavily starched pima cotton turquoise blouse. Even her gold hoop earring and gold necklace matched. Growing closer, he could hear her speaking to the officers. Her voice didn't quiver or crack. When she noticed movement, she turned her head and looked in his direction.

"Oh good, Alen! Thank you for coming." She said as she walked to him as gracefully as one would expect a southern woman to approach and welcome a guest in her home. *Joan was right, something sure smells fishy*, Alen thought.

Any other person, he would have hugged, but knowing Marsha, he took her hand and gently squeezed it. She pulled it away immediately.

Alen spoke softly, "Marsha, I'm so sorry! Can you tell me what happened?"

"Uh...sir, I'm questioning Mrs. Colfax. Can you wait inside for us to finish, please?"

Alen reached into his pocket and pulled out his credential's wallet, opened it and showed the officer his badge. He took Marsha's elbow and guided her back to her chair and pulled it out for her to sit. Then he sat in the chair next to her. Ignoring the officers sitting across from her, he said, "Marsha, tell me everything."

Chapter Three

"I was telling that officer over there. Did I thank you for coming?"

Well, at least that's something, Alen thought. If she didn't remember that, she wasn't as composed as she came across.

"Yes, you thanked me. Tell me, what was going on last night? Joan said something about a party?"

"Of course, we weren't having a party! If we were, you two would have been invited! But I may have misspoken when I was talking to Joan. I didn't know it was her. I forgot she worked for dispatch; you know. I was trying to call you. It was an automatic response I guess that I dialed 911, instead of your number. That is what people are supposed to dial in an emergency, right? Though,

11

technically, I suppose it wasn't an emergency, since he was dead. No hurry, right?"

"Well, yes, that's still an emergency, and you did the right thing to call 911. So, what was going on here last night?"

"George never came to bed last night. I thought he fell asleep out here in a lounge chair after everyone left. He thinks I don't know that he comes out here to smoke. I always let him believe I didn't know. It was just easier that way."

"I'm pretty sure he knew that you knew. He respected you for not raising a fuss. And when you woke up you came looking for him?"

"Well, first, I took a shower, then came down to get my coffee. My coffee wasn't ready. He always makes the coffee in the morning, because he's always the first one downstairs. But there was no coffee. That's when I started thinking he must have drunk too much with the boys last night and was still sleeping. So, I had to make the coffee. After that, I mean after it was ready and I had my cup of coffee, I came out here. I usually drink my first cup out here. I didn't see him. I assumed I missed him and he was in the house. You know at our age, the first thing that happens is we must visit the little girls' and boys' room."

"Yes, ma'am. I know all about that too. So, where were you sitting this morning to drink your coffee."

"Where I always do, of course. There on that settee. See, the newspaper is still there. I sat there looking out at the beautiful blue sky, and my flowers. Like I do every morning. You know, Alen, it's important to find something to be grateful about, every day. So, every morning, I drink my coffee out here, and I'm thankful for my beautiful morning space. That's how I start each day so positive."

"Yes, ma'am. That's a lovely way to start the day. Go on. What happened next?"

"Well, George never showed up. I was hoping he would, so he could get me a coffee refill. But he didn't. I went inside to fill my cup myself, and I called out to him. But he didn't answer. I checked the bathroom and he wasn't there. I thought maybe he went up to get in the shower before coming out to the deck. I came back out here, and I walked over there to the railing and that's when I saw him. Floating in the pool."

"I'm so sorry, that must have been awful for you."

"No. Not really. Not at all. I thought he was playing with me. You know, how he is. Such a jokester. Even after 28 years together, his jokes were annoying, but he thought they were funny. I yelled down to him. I said, 'George! Come out of the pool! Why didn't you make the coffee?' Of course, he didn't respond. He didn't move. So, I went down there. I got the skimmer net on the pole thingy and pushed him with it. He just kept floating. He looked funny. It felt funny pushing him all around the pool. I kept thinking any minute he was going to jump up out of the water, gasping for breath. He had been holding his breath for an awfully long time. And I knew when he did, he was going to scare me to death. And then it occurred to me that he had his clothes on."

She stopped speaking and reached for a glass of water. She took three small lady-like sips and no one moved or spoke. Alen noticed out the corner of his eye that the officer was frantically scribbling notes. He had a lot of questions in his mind too, but he didn't want to break Marsha's concentration of telling the story. This first telling would be the most important, and no one wanted to disturb her.

"I yelled at him then. I said, 'George! Get out of the pool. You've got your clothes on and that pool water will fade them and ruin them. I just bought that shirt. Hurry up, I'll go rinse them out.' But he kept floating and floating and not answering me. And then I noticed his shoes. Well...his shoe. One shoe on and one shoe off. I thought that was really odd. Why would someone get in a pool with one shoe on and one shoe off? Then I saw the other one on the bottom of the pool. I guess it fell off. I started poking him some more. I was mad then. I suppose that's when the coffee kicked in and I realized it. He wasn't kidding around. No one can hold their breath that long. And I knew he must be dead. I thought about dialing 911 and realized I was still in my housecoat and my hair had to look a fright, since I was fresh from the shower and all. I went upstairs and prepared myself to receive company. Then I called 911. That's how we ended up here in this moment."

"Mrs. Colfax," the officer began, but Alen raised a hand to silence him.

"Marsha, you said you thought he might have had too much to drink with the boys last night. Who was here with him? Did you have company?"

"No, I didn't have company. He did. If I had company, I wouldn't have gone up to my room to read and fell asleep."

"Of course. Do you know who was here with him?"

"Yes, what kind of wife would I be if I didn't know who he was entertaining?"

"I didn't mean any disrespect, Marsha."

"Oh, I know you didn't. It's irritating to have to answer all these personal questions in front of strangers. Yes, I know the officers are over there listening and taking notes. It's so dreadful to have to have our private lives exposed at such an emotional time."

Alen nodded. He never saw Marsha in an emotional state. Not of any kind. Today was no exception, so he wasn't sure why she called it an emotional time. But he sat and waited to see if she would get around to answering his question without him having to ask it again. She didn't disappoint him.

"Last night was the monthly poker game. It was all the gentlemen from the council."

"The city council?" asked the officer.

"Yes. They play poker once a month. Always on the second Tuesday night. They were all here last night. Usually the game ends about eleven. They don't want any ladies around, so I make them some snacks and I retire to my sitting room upstairs."

"Do they always play here, at your house? Or do they rotate turns hosting the game?" Alen asked her.

"Oh, it's always here. George said the other wives are terrible cooks. Some of them have children too. George didn't like being around children. So, they always played here."

"Did anyone else know about the game?"

"How on earth would I know that?"

"You're right, you wouldn't know that, would you? Is there anyone I can call to come stay with you?"

"No. If we're done here, I suppose I need to contact a funeral home and begin making arrangements. I'll call my friend Marjorie to come over and help organize things. My housekeeper comes today too, she should be arriving any minute."

"Okay, these officers will stay with you until someone comes. I don't want you here alone, okay."

"Why on earth not? I'm fine here by myself."

"We need to find out if George died of natural causes or if there was foul play. You shouldn't be alone until we figure it out."

"You should know, it was foul play."

"Why do you say that?"

"Well, first of all, George passed his executive physical last month with flying colors. The doctor said he had the body of a man twenty years younger than he is. I mean, was. And, there's an envelope inside. He said that if anything ever happened to him, I should give the envelope to you. He trusted you more than anyone else we knew. You know that, right?"

"Where is the envelope?"

"Inside, in his desk. Taped underneath the center drawer. Come with me, I'll show you."

Marsha rose, and all three men followed her silently into the house. She led them up the winding staircase that was the centerpiece of the two-story entry, to the third door on the right. Alen wasn't sure what the function of the second officer was or why he was tagging along everywhere. He never spoke. No introduction was made. Normally he would have introduced himself, but at the moment he didn't care who the guy was. Probably a trainee or probie. Marsha opened the door to George's office, went to the desk, pulled out the center drawer, felt underneath until she grasped the envelope, and she pulled it out. There was tape on the two long sides that came out with the envelope. She handed it to Alen. He noticed her hands were as steady as a surgeon's. He looked at her face before looking at the envelope. She had a dour look on her face, but the expression in her eyes seemed more like one of triumph. Like she was proving herself right. It was odd, but he didn't allow himself to dwell on it. He looked down at the envelope but he didn't reach for it.

He turned to the officers behind him. "Either of you have a pair of gloves?"

The first officer reached into his pocket and pulled out two latex gloves and handed them to the sheriff. Once he had the gloves on both hands, he took the envelope from Marsha.

He looked it over, on both sides. There was no writing, the envelope looked clean. He carefully opened it and withdrew a single sheet of paper. On it were only four words handwritten on the paper. After he read it, he looked up at Marsha and said, "You know, Marsha. You really should have led with this."

16

Chapter Four

"What does it say?" Marsha asked.

"Yeah, Sheriff, what does it say?" The detective asked.

Everyone turned to see a newcomer in the doorway. The man was in a suit. Alen slowly, slid the paper back into the envelope.

"I'm Detective Olsen. I'm sorry for your loss, Ma'am. Sheriff, what does it say?"

"Oh, nothing important. It was a personal message to me. It doesn't have anything to do with anything." Alen responded. "I'm going to the hospital to make sure they do an autopsy." He turned to Marsha, "If you need anything, anything at all, call me. I'll talk to you later."

"Uh, Sheriff, with all due respect, we need to know what that paper says." The detective said.

"I don't want an autopsy performed." Marsha blurted.

"The paper is not important; it's a note cancelling a loan from when I borrowed some money from George years ago."

"How long ago did your husband tell you about this envelope, Mrs. Colfax?"

"I don't remember, it's been a while, maybe a few months ago. Could've been a year ago. I don't know. That's why I didn't think about it right away."

"It's conceivable that note could implicate you, Sheriff, as a suspect. If it's determined that foul play was involved," the detective said.

"No." Alen and Marsha both said at the same time.

"Alen paid that loan back years ago. I guess the note's been there longer than I thought," Marsha said.

"With all due respect ma'am, that's your word, against potentially anyone else's. That letter needs to be admitted into evidence."

"We don't even know if there is any crime committed yet! George may have died from natural causes. Maybe he had a heart attack. Marsha, this is why we need an autopsy." Alen said.

"Oh, yes, I understand. Okay. That's okay with me, then. Can you see to all that? I don't know anything about how all this works." Marsha said.

The detective and the officer looked at each other, and then they both turned to Alen.

"It looks like we have a conflict of interest here. And I'm sorry, Sheriff. We can't let you leave with a potential piece of evidence."

Alen had to think fast. He knew what the officer and the detective were thinking and saying was right. But he didn't know who he could trust with the bombshell inside the envelope. Of course, it had nothing to do with him. Except that George had trusted him with the information. In the wrong hands it could be disastrous. Actually, he didn't want to believe it himself. But how was he going to get out of this situation. The room was beginning to look like a standoff in an old western. Except instead of standing on a dusty road, they were standing on a fine Turkish carpet. Instead of being surrounded by raw pine buildings, they were surrounded by bookshelves housing a collection of leather-bound books and first editions. Instead of two gunmen about to go a round over Miss Kitty, there were four law enforcement officers and a member of Corpus Christi society all staring at each other. And they were all wondering the same thing. How was this standoff going to end?

"The first thing we need to know was if there was even a crime, before we start throwing words like evidence around." Alen said, trying to sound like a voice of reason.

The two other law enforcement professionals looked at him. The officer even cocked his head as if to say, really Sheriff? The detective shook his head, and began to laugh.

"Detective! That is not appropriate! You're in the company of a lady whose husband just died."

"I'm sorry, ma'am. No disrespect intended. But it seems we may have a standoff here."

"Look. This letter doesn't really implicate me. But it does implicate someone important, *if* there was a crime here. But we don't know yet. If I let anyone else see this, and there was no crime, an influential person's reputation could be sullied unnecessarily."

"Oh, and we're just supposed to take your word for it?" the detective questioned.

"I see your point. So how do we resolve this? I mean I am considered a law-abiding citizen; the people trust me. The courts trust me. I've taken a sworn oath to uphold the law. So why can't you trust me?"

"Because you said it was a respected member of our community who is implicated in that envelope. Is that person not trusted? Have they taken any kind of oath? Who are you protecting, Sheriff, if not yourself?"

"There appears to only be one way to handle this quagmire. We need to call and see if the M.E. has determined cause of death. Maybe we don't have to wait for an autopsy." Alen said as he pulled his phone out of his pocket and placed a call.

"This is Sheriff Arny. I'm calling about George Colfax. Can you tell me when the M.E. might be able to determine the cause of death? I see. Yes. Thank you." He waited for a few seconds and then began again. "This is Sheriff Arny. I'm calling about George Colfax. When will you have a cause of death? Uh huh. Yes. I see. Thank you, Doctor." He hung up and turned to the officer and detective.

"Could Mrs. Colfax and I have the room for a few moments, please?" he asked them.

"Can't you tell us all what he said?"

"No. Not until I have a chance to talk to the widow first. Do you think we're going to roll up the carpet and use it to scale out the window? You can stand right outside the door."

"What is it, Alen? Just tell me, I don't care if the insensitive buffoons are here. Tell me. Please. Oh, I'm sorry, was that impolite? I really don't care. Alen, tell me."

"The cause of death was blunt force trauma. He was dead before he went into the pool."

"Well, this changes everything now, doesn't it?"

Alen handed the envelope to the detective. The detective pulled on a pair of gloves before taking the envelope. He pulled the paper out and showed it to the officer. The four words on the paper were: The Mayor did it.

Chapter Five

The detective took the paper and envelope and put them into an evidence bag. Without a word to anyone, both the officer and the detective left the room. Alen walked over to the window. It overlooked the pool area where the crime scene team was wrapping up their evidence collection and photographing. The detective asked the techs some questions. And then he left through the privacy fence gate.

Alen knew the windows of the upstairs rooms on the other side of the house provided a beautiful view of the bay. He also knew Marsha maintained her office on the front of the house.

Marsha was still standing in the center of the room, watching Alen. He was a bit over six feet tall, in good physical shape, without the belly paunch George developed over the last couple of years. He kept a clean-shaven head and she had wondered in the past if it was habit from being in the Marines or if it was to hide a bald spot. Today, she errantly thought of Howie Mandel and that he shaved because of extreme OCD and germaphobia. Alen struck her as neat, clean, but she'd never seen signs of anything extreme. Her money was on some pattern of baldness that shaving masked. She had not seen the note and didn't know what had everyone lurching into action. But she did wonder now, what on earth was wrong with her, that her husband was dead and she was thinking about Howie Mandel and Alen's bald head.

Alen's phone rang. He pulled it out of his pocket and looked at the screen. It was Joan. He answered it.

"Hi."

"Hi, what's going on? How is Marsha? What can I do?"

"I'm still here with Marsha. We just got word his death was not natural."

"I'm so sorry, Honey. I'm off duty. I wondered if I should come there to the house, go somewhere else, or go home. What does Marsha need?"

Alen turned to Marsha. "Joan is off duty would you like her to come here and stay with you for a while? Help you sort things out?"

"Yes, please. That would be so kind of her."

"Sweetheart, she said yes," Alen spoke low into the phone and turned away from Marsha. She was beginning to look a little bit shocky. He assumed it was all beginning to sink in, that her husband of 28 years was gone. "Could you stop and pick up some food on the way? I suspect Marsha hasn't eaten today."

"Sure, I'm on my way."

"Drive safe."

"I will. Don't leave before I get there. I'm bringing you food too. And I need to see you before you jet off to solve the case. I know you think you can do it better than anyone but you can let them do a little of the leg work. I'll be there in less than 30 minutes."

"I suspect that the other officers have already taken off on a fool's errand. I'll be here."

He hung up and walked over to Marsha. He wanted to hug her. But on a good day, Marsha was too stoic for a hug. And Alen knew if she was anything like his wife, a hug right now might dissolve all the composure she was fighting to maintain. So, he took her hand in his and gently placed his other hand under her elbow and quietly spoke to her.

"Joan is on the way, and she's bringing us something to eat. Why don't we go someplace comfortable to sit and we can talk if you feel like it until she gets here."

She started walking as he guided her out of her husband's office towards the stairs.

"Where would you like to sit?"

"In the music room, please. The windows look out front instead of over the pool."

The curtains were still drawn in the music room. The grand piano sat in the back corner and there were a couple of sofas and some overstuffed chairs. Although they called it the music room and it housed the grand piano, one wall of this room was also bookcases laden with classic and modern books. Joan sat on one of the sofas, Alen turned on the lamp on the round drum table next to the sofa and walked to the window to open the curtains. When he opened them, he noticed a throng of people congregated in the yard across the street. The nosy neighbors. He opted to leave the window covered, knowing the curious spectators would upset Marsha. Instead he turned on the other lamps around the room to brighten the area. Then he sat down across from Marsha.

"Do you feel like talking, Marsha? I have a few more questions about last night if you're up to it."

"Yes, of course, but I wonder, could you get me a glass of water from the kitchen? I feel absolutely parched."

"Yes, I can do that, I'll be right back. Is there anything else I can get for you?"

"No, that will be all."

When he returned, he noticed that Marsha looked like she had suited up in armor while he was out of the room. Her tired, slumped appearance from a couple of moments before was replaced with her normal staunch posture. Like a dog shaking off water, she looked composed and ready for anything.

"Marsha, you said all the councilmen were here last night for a regularly scheduled event."

"Yes, that's right. They aren't a very sophisticated lot, those men, when they play their poker. I made bruschetta and oatmeal chocolate chip raisin cookies for them to snack on. George always insisted they have finger food and nothing too messy, so the cards wouldn't get dirty. George always served as the bartender. I would greet them when they arrived and say hello. Then they would go to the deck to play cards and I would go upstairs to read or watch movies. It was a bit unusual for me to fall asleep before George came to bed, but last night I did."

"Do you know if anyone else came by the house? Maybe arrived later?"

"No. I don't think so, though if they didn't ring the bell and it was after I fell asleep, I might not have heard them. Why do you ask?"

"I'm trying to figure out if there might be a suspect other than one of the council members."

"Oh dear, I haven't thought of that. It will be terrible if one of them is who killed George. He thought of them all as friends. But, you know, George should have sought a higher political office, because he thought everyone was a friend. It didn't matter to him what their social status was. As long as they were voting age. The man didn't like children at all as you know. He said that's why he could never be a governor, senator, or president. He couldn't bring himself to be part of the "kissing baby brigade", as he called it."

Alen chuckled lightly, because he knew it was expected. He had heard the line many times over the years. But something still had him puzzled. In his line of work, throughout the years, and especially his time as a career Marine, he watched the different methods of how people reacted in times of tragedy and grief. He knew Marsha well enough to know she was from the old guard of Southern women who didn't air their dirty laundry outside the home, didn't show emotion, and cared too much what everyone thought of them. But even at that, how she was coping and dealing with this whole mess was puzzling. The phone rang. There wasn't a landline phone extension in the music room. But they could hear the ring in stereo from the other parts of the house.

"Oh my! I forgot Lucinda should have been here. Today is her day to clean. I better answer that, she never misses work. I wonder if she's sick or something..." she was still saying as she walked out of the music room toward the kitchen to answer the phone.

Alen followed her to listen in on whatever conversation she was about to have, hoping she wouldn't notice him eavesdropping.

"Hello?"

"Oh, hi Melanie. Yes, I'm okay."

Alen knew that Melanie was Marsha's younger sister. She was eight years younger, and Marsha felt she was weak. She wasn't the old school stoic, prim, and proper generation that Marsha was. Therefore, Marsha felt she was whiney and emotional about most things.

"It's on the news already? Really, is there no decency left? Yes, yes, that will be fine, thank you. I'll see you shortly."

No sooner did she click the button to disconnect the call, the phone began to ring again.

"Hello?"

"Lucinda! Where are you? Why didn't you come to work?" There was a short pause and then, "Oh, I see. Well, Alen is here and I'm sure he can take care of that. Could you please come back? The house needs to be cleaned, as you know. There are all kinds of people traipsing through here. Oh- hold on a minute, Alen is waving at me."

"Marsha, actually, don't have her come. We have to leave the house because it's a crime scene. And she can't clean until the police finish their investigation. We're waiting until Joan gets here. She can take you someplace to stay while they work in the house."

"Lucinda, stay at home. I'll call you back," Marsha said before hanging up the phone and turning to Alen.

"But, Alen, I don't want to leave my house. Especially not with strangers roaming around. I need to be here to protect my things."

"You don't have a choice, Marsha. It's standard procedure. I've already allowed you to stay here too long. Unfortunately, you can't even take anything out of the house. As soon as Joan comes and you eat something, we have to leave. I'm seriously bending some rules as it is. You need to go to the station. Since you were here when the crime occurred, they have to take a statement from you."

"You can't think I had anything to do with George's murder, can you?"

"No, I don't. But that doesn't matter. There are procedures and we have to follow them."

"Melanie said she was coming over; I'll call her and tell her not to come. How long until I can come back?"

"It might be hours or it could be weeks. It all depends on how the investigation goes."

"How do I know how much to pack?"

"Marsha, you can't pack. We'll have to get you some new things. Joan can help with that. Maybe you can stay with Melanie until they clear the house and you can return."

"Oh no. No, no, no, no, no. I cannot stay at my sister's house. She would send me round the bend in no time atall. I'll have to stay at a hotel. I can take my purse, can't I? I need my credit cards."

"You can take your wallet. That's all." Alen's phone rang. It was Joan.

"Honey, I'm here, but the officers won't let me in. Can you come tell them I'm not a suspect or something."

"I'm on my way."

To Marsha he said, "Marsha, try not to touch anything, sit there at the table, Joan is here, I have to get the officers to let her in. As soon as you eat, we'll go with you to the station. And then get what you need and help you get settled wherever you need to go."

Chapter Six

Alen opened the car door for his wife, took the bag of food from her, and took her hand to help her out of her car. Then he kissed her. He lingered near her ear and whispered.

"Hello, my beautiful wife. It's good to see you. But I need a favor. Someone needs to take Marsha down to the station for her statement, then she's going to need to go to a hotel and she will need some clothes and whatever else she needs to stay there a while. Can you handle all that? If you can, I can get started working on who killed George."

"Yes, of course, I can do that. You do what you need to do, I'll take care of Marsha. Then I'll see you at home later?"

Joan looked tall standing next to most women but she was a good eight inches shorter than her husband. She had auburn hair, a bit shorter than shoulder length and it had a natural wave to it that made it look bouncy, no matter what her mood was. She was above average height for most women at 5'6" but standing next to her husband one was apt to call her a pixie. Her smile caused her eyes to twinkle in an impish way. But they weren't sparkling today.

They walked into the house together. Joan opened up the bag of aromatic barbeque sandwiches and fries and laid out a spread for them, complete with napkins. Alen reminded her on the way into the house not to touch anything. Marsha's prints would already be all over the house. It appeared that the crime happened in the back yard, but the crime scene crew still wanted to inspect the interior of the house. The fact was, Marsha would be considered the prime suspect until she wasn't.

"Dear, thank you for bringing food. I'm sure your poor husband is famished; I've kept him tied up here so long. I can't remember the last time I ate fast food. It smells delicious."

They didn't talk, they focused on eating. Alen picked up the trash from the meal carefully and placed it all in the bag to take out with him.

"Marsha, where is your wallet? You need to get it, and Joan is going to take you to the police station to make your statement, and then to get you settled. I'm going to see what I can find out about the investigation, okay?"

"You know, this whole thing proves I did the right thing."

"What? What do you mean, Marsha? What did you do?" Alen sounded almost panicked thinking that Marsha was about to confess to having been a part of George's demise.

"If I called 911 as soon as I knew George was dead, I would now be going to the police station, shopping for clothes, and checking into a hotel in my housecoat. I'm sure glad I took the time to make myself presentable before I called 911."

Relieved, Alen and Joan both let out the breath they were holding.

"The officers would have allowed you to get dressed, I promise."

"Well, wouldn't that allow me time to hide the murder weapon?"

Alen and Joan froze and looked at Marsha.

"Oh, for heaven's sakes, I meant if I had killed him. I don't understand why they would let me get dressed, if I wasn't, but they won't let me pack a suitcase."

Alen walked them out to Joan's car. He kissed his wife, thanked her, and then jogged to his own car to head to the medical examiner's office.

In Joan's car, she opened her glove box and pulled out a small notebook and pen. She handed them to Marsha.

"Make a list of your sizes, and what toiletries you need for a day or two. While you're giving your statement, I can run to the store and pick up a few things for you."

"Oh, that's okay. I can make that easy. I have a personal shopper who already knows what I like and has my credit card on file. I can call her and tell her what I need, then you can pick it up from her, no need to pay or anything."

"Okay, that's a great idea! Tell me where to go to pick it up and when it will be ready."

Marsha pulled her phone out of the inside of her big wallet and pushed a button.

"Sherry, this is Marsha Colfax. I need a few things please. My friend Joan will come to pick them up. Here's what I need, I need two day-wear outfits, one lounge outfit, a nightgown, a house coat, and some house shoes. I need the full battery of all my makeup, skin care, and hair products. Whatever you select should go with my black shoes, please. Oh, and I need a new handbag, a pair of sunglasses, a neutral scarf, and some costume jewelry to go with the day outfits. Please buy a suitcase and put it all in there. That should do it for now. Thank you. When will it be ready? Perfect, add a $10 tip to your fee when you run the charge please. Joan will be there in about an hour, then."

Joan escorted Marsha into the station where they were directed to the detective who was at the house earlier.

"Hello, Mrs. Colfax, I'm detective Olsen again. I was at the house earlier."

"Yes, I remember your burliness, I just didn't remember your name."

"Come this way. I need to take your statement. Your friend can wait out here."

"I'm going to run an errand, and then I'll be back here waiting." Joan told him.

It was 8:20 that night, when Alen heard Joan's car pull into the garage. He was on the phone talking to one of his deputies and tried to wrap up the call. When he hung up, he heard Joan talking to someone. She never talked on the phone while driving, so he wondered who she was talking to. He thought maybe a neighbor, but he remembered hearing the garage door close.

The door to the kitchen opened and Joan walked in, still talking, to Marsha. Marsha was wheeling a new looking suitcase behind her.

"Hi, Honey. I invited Marsha to stay with us until they clear her house. I figure it shouldn't take too long, but I couldn't leave her all alone at a hotel." Joan explained quickly to avoid Alen asking any embarrassing questions.

"What a fine idea! Welcome to our home, Marsha."

The Arny's home was much less formal, less sprawling, and far less opulent than the Colfax home. It was a taupe colored, sided house with a deep red roof and trim. It had a large master suite upstairs with a small attic above, and the rest of the house was on the ground floor. The house was situated at the back edge of a two-acre yard. Alen sodded and kept about half of it in front of the house and the smaller backyard area cut and manicured. The outer edges were typical Texas scraggly with a fair amount of clover, wild onions, and low growing tiny wild flowers he had yet to tame and eradicate from the yard. But it was plenty big for the two of them.

One of the things that Joan and Alen had in common with Marsha and George is that neither couple had children. One of the many things they didn't have in common was that Joan and Alen felt this house was more than enough space for them, while the Colfaxes needed three times the amount of space. In all fairness, Marsha and George did a lot more entertaining, and they employed help to maintain the house and rambling landscape. Alen and Joan spent the majority of their time at work.

"I'm going to show her to the guest room, we'll be right back. Have you eaten?"

"Yes, I have. I'll be right here," Alen said as he sat at the kitchen table.

"Good. Marsha enjoyed the barbecue sandwich so much for lunch, we stopped for another before going to the hotel."

Joan took Marsha to the guest room.

Alen wondered at that statement. *If they went to a hotel, how did they end up with Marsha staying in their guest room?*

"Joan, thank you for having me here and taking care of that unfortunate problem with my credit card. I'll call them first thing tomorrow and get it straightened out. But I hope you and Alen don't mind, I would like to turn in for the evening. It's been a grueling day."

"Sure, you do whatever you need to do. We're here if you need us, but we will give you some space."

Joan returned to the kitchen and put on a pot of coffee before sitting down at the table with Alen.

"Something truly doesn't feel right about this whole situation." She told him.

"You mean that our friend is dead? Or that his wife hasn't shed a tear? Or that other than said wife, the primary suspects are the entirety of the City Council?"

"Well, yes, all those things. Add to that, she called her private shopper to get the things she needed. And when I went to pick it up her credit card was declined. I paid the bill at the department store with our credit card. Two days' worth of clothes, make up, and such was over $1500. And then when I took her to the hotel all three of her credit cards were declined. I sure hope she's not guilty and can pay us back!"

"Hmm, yes that does raise some questions doesn't it? I have a few more calls to make. Are you okay?"

"Yeah, I'm fine. It's days like this I still really miss my sweet Zoey."

"I know, me too. I miss having a dog. But the loss is too hard, I don't think I could bare to lose another one."

"You know, it's been years. It could be worth it to do it again. They bring so much love. There's nothing like a happy pet greeting you every time you come in the door." She told him as she fixed them each a cup of coffee.

"Not yet, Joan. It still hurts. No dog could replace her. I'll be in the office. I promise, only a few quick phone calls."

"Since Marsha went to bed, I think I'll go to our bedroom too. I'll see you when you're done."

She curled up in the arm chair with a book and waited for her man to come to bed. She hoped the book would temporarily take her mind off the death of their friend. But her overactive imagination wasn't going to have it. She was wondering who in the world would want George Colfax dead. And why were their credit cards not working?

Alen finally came to bed after another hour on the phone.

"What's happening? Do you know anything yet?" Joan asked him as she rose from her chair and joined him on the side of the bed. She snuggled up as close to him as she could get, looped her arm under his and laced her fingers through his, and kissed him gently on his temple. She knew he hadn't had an opportunity to process the loss yet. And she didn't know if it was better for him to process it now or stay busy.

"Of course, no one will tell me much. I'm excluded from the investigation. I suppose I'm lucky I'm not a suspect. Yet. All I know is he died from blunt force trauma to the head. He died before he hit the water. I just can't imagine what happened. Why anyone would try to kill him. What he could have done to deserve this. Or was it an accident? That just looks like murder. I mean the note didn't say *what* the mayor did."

"What note? The mayor? Marsha said there was a party, but we weren't invited. That's unusual. Who was there? What kind of accident?"

Alen explained to her all the information and explanations he had received at the Colfax's home before she came to take Marsha away.

"So, what do you think happened? Can you come up with a logical scenario for it to be accidental?" she asked.

"Not really. Short of someone dropping an anvil off the deck onto his head and him stumbling into the pool. But there was no blood, except in the pool. No anvil laying around. I suppose someone could have cleaned up after themselves, but who, and why? And why does Marsha not seem upset at all?"

"Yeah, Marsha is odd, even for Marsha. But we know, everyone deals with grief differently. Maybe it hasn't sunk in for her yet. I mean, it's hard for me to wrap my mind around it. What about you? Are you okay?"

"Yeah, I'm fine as long as I stay busy. I know I'll have to deal with it soon. But if I can stay focused on the investigation, I won't have to deal with it now. Since I can't really do that, I don't know."

Alen stood up and got ready for bed. Joan walked around to her side of the bed and climbed in. He snuggled next to her and she stroked his head until he fell into a fitful sleep. She started to wonder. She didn't want to have these thoughts, but was sure until she found a way to dispel them, there would be no sleep in the near future for her. She silently hoped that the same thought wouldn't occur to Alen and that somehow, she could find the proof she needed without his help. She needed desperately to find a way to answer the question she felt was the most important...was the woman sleeping down the hall a killer?

Chapter Seven

The only time Alen and Joan had together over the next few days was in their bedroom at bedtime. Even though Marsha was staying with them, Alen was gone until late in the evening trying to discover what had happened to his friend, without appearing to meddle in the investigation. Even though Joan worked for dispatch and theoretically was in the law enforcement field, Alen never shared details with her of ongoing investigations. She was used to having to be patient and wait until an investigation was complete before he could give her the details. Sometimes she got more information from the evening news than from her sheriff husband.

Alen and Joan called themselves, "An island unto ourselves." They neither one had any family. They had friends and socialized. They loved trivia night and occasionally they would go with a group of friends to a karaoke night. They were each other's second marriage.

Every Friday night, unless Alen was working and couldn't get away, Alen and Joan went out to dinner. Sometimes just the two of them and sometimes with friends. Joan was afraid with Alen trying to secretly solve George's murder that he would try to cancel. But she thought it was important for them to have some time that felt normal. At least as normal as possible. They were scheduled to have dinner this week with the Mayor, Jim Ellis and his wife, Sophie.

Without asking Alen, she called Sophie to cancel.

"Sophie, I'm so sorry, but I need to reschedule our dinner plans. Alen is working until all hours trying to figure out what happened to George, and I feel we neither one will be good company tonight." she explained.

"I completely understand. The whole city council and Jim's office are chaos right now. No one seems to be functioning at capacity. Everyone is wondering if they could be in danger too? Was the murder because of the job? I mean why else would anyone kill sweet George? Do you know anything? Do they have any leads?"

Alarm bells went off in Joan's mind. Surely, Sophie wasn't asking for information about the investigation. She reminded herself that they were all curious, everyone wanted answers, and no one could understand and the question was likely one of frustration, not prying.

"No, I don't know anything. Alen never talks to me about ongoing investigations and this time, he's not really included in the process. I think he's kind of digging around behind the scenes, feeding questions and ideas to the investigators, but he's not allowed to work it. But doing what he's doing is helping him deal with the loss, I suppose. I know there is no way he could just sit on his hands. So, we are just waiting for it to all play out, like everyone else. Can I call you in a week or two to reschedule?"

"Absolutely, that will be fine."

Then Joan called her husband.

"Honey, it's Friday. We were scheduled to have dinner with Jim and Sophie, but I cancelled it. However, I hope you and I can still go out. I told Marsha already that we would be out tonight. I told her we could bring something back for her, but she said she would take care of her dinner."

"Oh darn! I wish you hadn't done that!"

"Done what?"

"Cancelled with Jim and Sophie. I would love an excuse to talk to him on the downlow, in a social situation. Get a feel for where his head is. Maybe break into what happened that night."

"What do you mean? Are you putting stock into the note? Do you really think Jim could have killed George? And why? Has anyone questioned him yet?"

"No, I don't think he killed George. At least I hope not. I can't imagine anyone we know being a killer. But he obviously did something for George to leave the note, right? I don't think anyone has questioned him yet. I wouldn't if I were leading the investigation. They need to find more proof, some connection or motive, because they will only get one chance to question him before they lose the element of surprise. From what I gather, they have talked to all the council members that were there that night. Every one of them confirms that he was still alive when they left. Now, they are looking for anyone else who might have a motive or reason to kill him, before they bring in the mayor. No one wants to do that if they are wrong."

"I'm sorry. Do you want me to call Sophie back?"

"No, no. That will be too suspicious."

"Okay, I was hoping to have some time with you. Just the two of us."

"You got it. I agree. It'll be nice. Maybe someplace quiet though. I'm not much in a mood for fun. But I am missing you, it seems like I've hardly seen you in days."

"Meet you at home? And go together from there?"

"Sure, I'll be home no later than 6:30. I'll call when I'm on the way. If you haven't heard from me by then, call me. In case I lose track of time."

"I will. I love you, stay safe."

"I will. You too."

His lack of saying I love you told Joan how distracted he was. He usually said it first. She wasn't worried about it, other than it told her he was still deep into the case and wondering.

She heard Marsha come out of her room. Since Joan worked four ten hour shifts a week, she was off today. She was dressed and ready for the day ahead. The police had returned Marsha's car to them the evening before after processing it looking for any evidence. Marsha was also dressed for the day, new purse in hand and was obviously on her way out. Joan had taken her to the funeral home yesterday and they made all the arrangements for the funeral which wouldn't be until at least Monday because the body wasn't released yet.

"What do you have planned today?" Joan asked Marsha as Marsha walked to the coffee pot and poured herself a cup.

"I have some errands to run. I'm out of anything to wear after today. I hope I will be able to get back into my house. But I suppose I need to go buy an outfit for tomorrow, just in case. I also have some other business to take care of. Aren't you working today?"

"No, I'm off today. Fridays are the day I do my grocery shopping, the dry cleaning, all those sorts of things. Is there anything I can do for you? Anything I can pick up for you?"

"No, dear. Thank you for asking. I can handle it. You said you and Alen will be out tonight, right? I'm going to have dinner with my sister, so I'll be home late too. Don't wait up for me, I can see myself in. Hmm, I suppose, do you have a spare key, so I don't have to bother you when I come in. "

"Yes, I pulled it out for you last night when they brought your car."

"Well, then, I'll be on my way. It's a busy day." Marsha said.

"I was just leaving too. We can walk out together."

How is it that woman's husband was murdered and she basically played with his dead body in the pool, and got ready for a day like it was a bridge game before calling 911? And hasn't shed a single tear? Joan wondered, as she prepared to follow this woman she was beginning to think of as a beast to see just exactly what she was up to.

At 6:10 Joan's phone rang. She clicked the button on her steering wheel that would route the call through her radio and she was driving out of the neighborhood where Marsha's sister apparently lived. She had been following the woman all day to see what important business the woman had two days after the death of her husband. The display on her dash told her it was Alen calling.

"Hi honey. How has your day been?"

"Frustrating. I'm on my way home."

"Oh, me too. I'm running a bit behind. I'll be there in about thirty minutes probably with the traffic. I'm sorry. It turns out I'm the one who lost track of time."

"Did you happen to get tonic at the grocery today? I could make myself a drink while I wait."

"Um, well no."

"It's okay, I'll have some juice, it's better for me in my present state of mind anyway."

41

"Honey, I'm so sorry, there's no juice either. Honestly, I didn't make it to the store yet. I'll go in the morning."

"What have you been up to all day? I don't mean that in a bad way!" He clarified realizing how the remark could sound. "I meant did you have fun? Go shopping, meet up with friends, go for a long jog?"

"None of the above. I'll tell you all about it at dinner. There is some sweet tea in the fridge. I'll be there as quick as I can and we can go, we could even have a drink before dinner if you want."

"I'm fine, I'll see you soon. And sweetheart?"

"Yes?"

"I love you!"

"I know."

Joan rushed into the house like she was late for an important date. Because, well, she was. Going out with Alen was still a special treat, even though they did it at least 52 times a year and had for almost 18 years. And tonight was extra special. Alen needed time away, time to process what he was going through, and time with his wife. They called this "shut down" time. No phones. No work talk. Sometimes they went out with friends, but usually it was the two of them.

She was glad she prepared for dinner before she left this morning. She wanted to know what Marsha was doing when left to her own devices, but she never dreamed it would take all day. Now she was wondering if her activities today would count as "work talk" or not. She decided on the drive home, that tonight was Alen's night. Whatever he needed was what would happen. If he brought up Marsha, maybe she would tell him. If not, it would wait. There wasn't anything too earth shattering to tell any way. She wasn't sure what she expected Marsha to do, or what she thought she would discover. But actually, the day was fairly innocuous.

Alen was standing at the kitchen window, looking out on the back yard, a mug of coffee in his hand.

"Hi Honey, I'm sorry I'm late."

"No problem, Sweetheart. I was thinking about all the times we talked about putting in a pool. I'm pretty glad we never did it."

"I'm sorry there was no tonic or juice here for you. I'll get to the grocery in the morning. Why is that? About the pool I mean?"

"I don't know. I think right now seeing a pool would make me think of George. Where do you want to go to dinner?"

"I was thinking about that. We were supposed to go out with Jim and Sophie at Romano's. Italian sounds good, but I figure since we cancelled and they might still go without us, we shouldn't go there."

"Let's go to Frank's."

"Perfect idea! I need to visit the little girl's room and I'm ready to go."

Frank's was Corpus Christi's oldest Italian restaurant, located in a house built in the 20s. They were family owned, served authentic Italian food, recipes passed down from Frank, a first-generation immigrant, in a quaint environment. It would be a quiet place where conversation would be easy for them.

Alen drove, but they went in Joan's SUV, instead of Alen's pick up, like they did every Friday night.

"So, tell me Sweetheart, since you didn't do your normal Friday errands today, what were you up to today?"

"Hmm, well, I think it might be a conversation that's off limits for date night."

"What on earth could that be?"

"It might be considered work related."

"Wow, that's unusual! You don't normally bring work home. Certainly not something that would occupy your day off. You've piqued my curiosity. But as per date night rules, I won't press.

Though I will say, Mrs. Arny, I love the mysterious side of you. I suppose, I'll have to suffer the curiosity until tomorrow."

Because date night rules were in effect through bedtime. They drove the rest of the way to Frank's in contemplative silence.

When they arrived, they asked for a quiet table if possible. They were ahead of the heavy dinner rush, so they were ushered to a quiet corner table. When the hostess laid the menu down, Alen said, "We don't need menus, we know what we want."

"Okay, I'll send your waiter right over to take your order then, sir. Enjoy your meal."

Joan looked at Alen and placed her hand, open palm up, on the table. Alen reached for it and closed his hand around hers. The waiter approached before either of them could even say anything.

"Good evening, are you ready to order?"

"Yes, thank you. My beautiful wife will have the famous Chicken Parmigiana and I'll have the Spaghetti please. A bottle of house red, too. And a glass of water for each of us."

"Yes, sir. I'll be right back with your wine and water."

They were still holding hands when he left the table. Joan looked at Alen with concern reflecting in her eyes.

He reached into his jacket pocket and withdrew a small box. He handed it to Joan.

"What is this?"

"It's just a little something I picked up, to say I'm sorry."

"Sorry for what?" She asked before opening the box.

"Well at the moment I bought it, I was sorry for criticizing you for cancelling our dinner tonight. You did what you thought, well, actually what is best for me, and you had no idea what I was thinking. I'm sorry. But I'm also sorry for all the turmoil in our lives this is causing."

"Neither of those is your fault, and there is no reason to apologize. But I do love presents."

She opened the box, and inside was a small brooch about the size of a strawberry. The center was a pure white pearl that formed the body of a frog. Protruding from the pearl body were four bright green enamel frog legs.

"Oh, Alen, it's so cute! Thank you, I love it." She immediately attached it to the lapel of the tan cotton jacket she was wearing. Joan was a collector of anything frog. But she turned her attention to her bigger concern at the moment. Her husband.

"How are you, honey? Are you okay?"

"Yeah, I'm fine. On one hand, I'm better that it wasn't natural causes, because that would threaten my mortality too, since we're the same age. But on the other hand, I can't imagine why this had to happen."

The waiter returned with their water, and poured them each a glass of wine. They didn't talk while he was there. Joan thanked him and he retreated from the table.

"I wonder if Marsha will sell the house, or stay there. I don't know what I would do, if something happened to you. I get wanting to stay, where it's familiar, and I get wanting to leave, because of being too familiar," Alen said.

"Yeah, I never thought about that. It would be a hard decision. I suppose all decisions after a death are hard."

"Well, I'm pretty sure if you were murdered at home, I wouldn't be able to stay there. Heck, I'm not sure I could even go in there at all."

"There is that. But I guess we don't know what we would do. Everyone reacts differently and I truly believe that we don't really know how we would act after a devastating or traumatic situation until it happens to us."

"I know. I keep trying to tell myself that. I mean, Marsha seems so strange."

"In all fairness, Marsha is always a little strange, in that she isn't like most people. Somehow, she manages most of the time to come across as welcoming and warm, and yet, she never reveals much of herself, and definitely not emotions."

"I know, and even taking all that into account, she still seems off somehow. What do you think? Is it something I should be concerned about? Do you think even for a minute, she should be considered suspect in his death?"

Now it was decision time for Joan. She had to decide whether to jump off into her own suspicions or adhere to the "date night" rules. She was afforded a few extra minutes to make the decision when the waiter approached to bring their salads.

"Honestly, I agree with you," she said, her decision made. This didn't feel like work talk as much as validating Alen's feelings over the loss of his friend. And that's what this night was all about in her mind.

"Something has seemed off ever since I took the 911 call. I've been curious about her actions and reactions through the whole thing. Since she had her car today and was free to go and do whatever she wanted, I decided to follow her."

"You did what? Lady, you never cease to surprise and amaze me. Before you tell me what she did today, tell me what piqued your curiosity enough to care so much about what she was doing to give up your day off following her around."

"I never got a chance to tell you about her 911 call. In almost 25 years of taking 911 calls it was one of the most bizarre calls I've ever taken. I've heard recordings of wild and crazy calls. But it was the strangest I've ever answered. And then she has seemed so unaffected by the whole thing ever since. Like the thing that upset her the most is the inconvenience of it all."

"What did you think she would do today?"

"Honestly, I figured her first stop would be the bank. She hasn't even mentioned again the $1500 I had to cover for her mini shopping spree. She's made no mention of paying us back. She did say this morning she needed more clothes. So, I thought maybe she would go shopping for more. And I was curious how she would pay for it."

"And is that what she did?"

"No. Neither of them. She drove to a coffee shop across town, like she knew exactly where she was going. Not like she was looking for a place to kill time," she grimaced as soon as the words left her mouth, knowing her pun loving husband would catch it immediately.

"I'm sorry! Poor choice of words!"

Alen laughed. It was the first time she had heard him laugh since Wednesday.

"Good one, Sweetheart!" he responded.

The waiter came to take away their salad plates and replace them with their entrees.

"Mmm, this looks delicious!" Joan said. "There's not much that melted ooey gooey cheese won't cure." But she knew that Alen needed comfort food. Spaghetti was his go-to comfort meal and she realized it as soon as he ordered it. He usually ordered the 1/2 Spaghetti 1/2 Ravioli plate. But tonight, was an all spaghetti night. She wondered if knowing that subconsciously was why she suggested Italian food tonight.

The conversation turned direction and lagged while they both dug into their meal.

"I didn't realize how hungry I was," Alen said between bites.

Joan almost said, me too, because she never ate all day, sitting in her car on an unofficial stakeout following Marsha, but she didn't want to be the one to turn the conversation back to that topic. So, she nodded agreement and kept eating.

47

A few minutes later, plates about half cleaned, Alen asked, "Want to split a rum drenched Tiramisu with me?"

Joan pretended to be in heavy contemplative thought for a moment and then responded, "No, I don't think so tonight." She paused, he looked up from his plate and looked her in the eye, surprised, and then she continued, "I think we should both have our own."

Alen chuckled, and it made Joan relax and filled her with warmth, the knowledge, that this was a hard time for Alen, but he would be okay, because he could still laugh.

Over dessert, Alen took the conversation back to Joan and Marsha's day.

"You said she went to a coffee shop."

"Oh yeah, not near our house, not near hers. Not like a usual haunt, but deliberate. She sat there until after lunch. A man joined her at 12:15. I didn't recognize him. They ordered lunch. They talked. Nothing seemed unusual other than her getting there three hours early and drinking coffee and her meeting a man just days after her husband's murder. He paid the lunch check and after he left, she left."

"Sweetheart, how do you know all this?"

"Duh! I was watching from the parking lot across the street. When something interesting would happen, I used my cell phone camera to zoom in on it."

"Color me dazzled. Continue, my gumshoe bride."

"She left and drove to the beach and sat in her car, apparently staring out at the waves until 5:30. Then she drove to her sister's house. She was still there when I came home. When I told her we were eating out tonight, she said she was eating at her sister's."

"How do you know it was her sister's house?"

"Well, because she went there at dinner. But Sheriff, you have a valid point. A woman greeted her at the door, but you're right. I don't know her sister, so it's possible it was someone else."

"So, what's your conclusion of Joan's day?"

"I'm perplexed why she didn't seem worried about the money."

"But you didn't see her spend any either. You said the man paid for lunch, likely the coffee she drank beforehand. She didn't go shopping for more clothes. Maybe she didn't go to the bank because she knew there was no money there."

"Then why did she order all that stuff? How did she think it would get paid for?"

"Sweetheart, I think you were played. It sounds like there are some financial problems afoot. I'll get someone to check on their finances tomorrow. Are you ready to go?"

"I am. I'm stuffed and miserable. Thank you, Honey, for a delicious dinner."

"Why are you thanking me? I thought you were paying. I didn't bring my wallet."

As he pulled her chair out for her, she punched him lightly on the arm, laughed and said, "Good thing I brought the credit card, huh?"

Chapter Eight

The police department with the letter found under George's desk drawer were focusing on their suspect, the mayor. They interviewed all the poker playing city council members, and were no closer to solving the mystery.

The sheriff couldn't actively work this investigation since the widow was now his house guest. But he did raise some questions for his detectives to investigate on the down low.

Questions like how much life insurance did George have? Were they in deep debt? If so, why? Had anyone close to the couple witnessed any domestic arguments? Was there a divorce looming? And while Detective Olsen was just sure that the note they found meant that the Mayor was involved in George's death, Alen realized the note didn't say what the mayor did, just that he did it. Was George leaving some other kind of encrypted message? And as the days went by, the funeral arrangements were made and the funeral took place, and Marsha was still inhabiting their guest room, with still nary a tear...he began to wonder if George was the one that left the note.

Monday morning, probably the most appropriate time to hold a funeral, Alen thought. *And raining to boot...just perfect.* He was dreading it like no other funeral. He'd never been a pall bearer before. Both of his parents were cremated. His mother had seen to all the details when his father died, and his aunt took charge when his mother died. He hadn't come home from Iraq. He could have, but he didn't see the point. They were dead. He had a job to do.

He dressed in a dark suit, and sat in the kitchen waiting for time to go. Joan went to work, but would take off and meet him at the funeral home. The visitation last evening was brutal. Funeral visitations were always brutal. But added to the uncomfortableness of the body of his closest friend laying in a metal box, looking most unnatural, his widow taking a receiving line of condolences and the awkward silences wondering what there was to say that would make any one feel better about this situation, Alen was looking at each and every face, wondering if there was a killer among them.

The funeral service was warm and heartfelt with the pastor from the First Baptist Church of Corpus Christi presiding. He told a few stories about how the councilman was always there to help out on service days around the church. How much he loved his wife. And how he would live in eternal peace through all of the days now.

Joan, sitting stoically next to Alen, their fingers entwined, their shoulders touching, wondered if all the same things could be said about Alen's widow. Sure, she served on the obligatory charity boards and committees. But did she love her husband? Joan found herself physically shaking at the thought of losing Alen.

He was the person she couldn't wait to go home to at the end of the day. The person she loved sleeping next to at night, and waking up to in the morning. She loved the occasional times they got out of the city for a day-long hike. But more than anything, he was her family. The person she had fun with, the person who understood when she was emotional to just hold her and let her cry. The person who she knew undoubtedly would support her in any dream she wanted to pursue. Right now, at this moment, as they prepared to lay to rest a man the exact age of her Alen, she was giving birth to a new dream. She didn't have the details yet for how to make it work or even what exactly it would look like. But she knew for certain, the time was now, for them to start really living life. It was a meme on social media, and she didn't know exactly what it meant, but if they were going to do it, it was time to get on with it, before it was too late.

Beside her, Alen was remembering the day he met the woman sitting beside him. It was a first responders charity event in December of 2001. Mere months after the devastation of the first terrorist attack on the country, 9-11, when emotions were high for the support of first responders, they were raising money for the college funds of the orphans left on that fateful day. No event in the city of Corpus Christi was as successful in raising funds. Alen was attending as a sheriff's deputy in his uniform, and Joan was working the table collecting the donations. She wore a black dress, and he was immediately attracted to her. He went over and took a hundred dollar check he was planning to donate, and when she smiled up at him, he had feelings and stirrings he hadn't felt in literally decades. His tongue tied like a Garfield cartoon cat. She thanked him, he simply nodded to her and stepped out of the way for the next patron to receive her lovely smile.

He walked out to his truck, unlocked the passenger side door, opened the glove box and removed his checkbook. He wrote another hundred-dollar check. All the way back into the building he rehearsed what he would say in his head. And when it was his turn, she looked up at him and instead of just saying thank you, she said, "Haven't I seen you here before?" His practiced line was blown.

Before the evening was out, he donated eight separate hundred-dollar checks, and finally knew her name.

The music began, alerting Alen it was time for him to walk to the front, and help carry his friend out of the church for the last time. He held on tight to the memory of that first meeting of Joan, to keep the threatening saline drops from escaping his burning eyes.

After Joan changed out of her dress clothes and slipped into a t-shirt and yoga pants, she went looking for Alen. He was sitting in the living room on the sofa and looked deep in thought.

"What's on your mind, handsome?"

"Hmmm, oh, just thinking about the funeral. It was nice, wasn't it?"

"As far as funerals go, yes, it was."

"You know, I really kind of missed most of it. I was thinking back to the night I met you. You remember how many checks I donated that night?"

"I do. Eight to be exact. I thought it was one of the most awkwardly romantic encounters I had ever had."

"Awkwardly romantic? Why awkward? I saw myself as dashing."

"Sir, you were not dashing. Cute. In that awkward puppy with a too heavy butt, or a foul's first steps kind of way. I thought you had a speech impediment the first three times you approached to make a donation."

"I did. I was tongue-tied, star struck, bewitched by the beauty behind the table. You could have been kind and asked me out."

"Oh, a lady never asks a gentleman out."

"It would have saved me several hundred bucks."

"But it all went to a good cause."

"That it did."

"You know what I was thinking during the funeral?"

"What?"

"I was wondering, again, obviously not for the first time, what all those memes I see on social media mean, when they say 'live life'. I mean, I'm quite sure they don't have all those lovely pictures and flowery words to encourage us to go to work, remember to put gas in the car, and buy groceries. They must be referring to more. And you know, we aren't getting any younger. I think we should talk about what living life means to us, if we were to start planning to fulfill some dreams."

"Okay. What do you think it means?"

"I think it means spending time doing things you love. Maybe trying new things. Having fun. I think we don't make enough time for that."

"What do you mean? We have date night every week. We go hiking from time to time. And you only remember to buy gas about every third tankful, so what are you complaining about?"

She laughed at his joke. Though it wasn't really a joke. About every other week, Joan ran out of gas and had to call for assistance. It was the primary reason they enrolled in AAA. So that if Alen was working a case and couldn't assist her she didn't stay stranded somewhere. He took her car and filled it up for her once a week, but about twice a month she managed to run out of gas anyway. They had made a pact to neither one feel like a failure because of it. It was just Joan being Joan.

"I know. We do things occasionally. But what about big dreams? Like bucket list stuff. Maybe we should make a bucket list."

'Okay, get some paper, let's make one."

"I want to go sky diving."

"Are you nuts?"

"No, adventuresome. What do you want to do?"

"Go fishing."

"Seriously, Alen, nothing more adventuresome than that?"

"I don't mean lake fishing; I mean deep sea fishing."

"There you go! That's what I'm talking about! I want to go to places I've never been to before, and do things I didn't even know were things."

"Well, write that on the list...do things I don't even know are things. I'm not sure how we'll plan for that, but put it on the list."

"I'm betting if I go to places I haven't been to before, I'll discover the things I didn't know about. Like going to Alaska and running the Iditarod. Yeah, I know that's a thing, but in faraway places they will have things I don't know about."

"I understand, now."

"So, what else do you want to do?"

"I want to follow a beautiful lady as she explores. Can it be my bucket list to just be your groupie? Can I adventure vicariously through your unknown activities?"

"Hmm, I don't know. I'll think about it. That does seem a bit stalkery, doesn't it?"

"Is stalkery a word?"

"It is now, I just used it. Let's see. If you want to be my groupie, I think it should begin with," she said as she picked up her phone and started pushing buttons.

"Delivered pizza?" he asked hopefully.

The notes of *Unchained Melody* came pouring from the phone speaker.

"You should dance with me," she said.

And he did.

Then he picked up his phone and started pushing buttons.

"You're going to play another song?" she asked, surprised. Alen didn't like to dance, and never ever under any circumstances would he dance in public. But from time to time in the privacy of their home, he would.

"Nope," he responded, with a crooked smile and a gleam in his eye he said, "I'm ordering dinner. I'm hungry. But while Pizza Palace prepares and delivers our dinner, I have time for a couple more dances with my bride."

"Have I told you lately, how much I love that you still call me your bride? And that I love you?"

"Not lately enough," he said, as he pushed more phone buttons and the lyrics of *Wonderful Tonight* came through his phone. He pulled her close and she whispered, "I love you."

Chapter Nine

After a week and a day in their guest room, Marsha was allowed to return to her home. There had been no mention during the week about the $1500 credit card charge Joan had covered. Actually, there hadn't been much conversation at all. Once her car was cleared from the investigation and returned to her, she had her own transportation even though she couldn't return home. Alen and Joan would leave for work in the mornings before she came out of the guest room. When they came home in the evenings she wasn't there. She would come in as or after they were going to bed. Which obviously raised even more questions. When Joan got home that afternoon, again, Marsha's car was gone.

But there was a note on the kitchen counter. It simply said, *Thank you for your hospitality in this difficult time. I'm allowed to return home now; I'll talk to you soon. Marsha.*

Joan called Alen. He didn't answer and she left a message, not because he would listen to the message before he called her back. In fact, she knew he wouldn't. But it made her feel better to say it out loud.

"The mystery woman has returned to her home. We have our house back to ourselves. I'm cooking dinner for us. Please come home soon."

As expected, he did call her back, before listening to the message.

"Hi Sweetheart, what's up?"

"Marsha went home. We have our house back. Can you come home early? I'm cooking your favorites. I really need to spend some time with you."

"I'll do my best. I love you sweetheart. I think the case is about to break open."

"I love you too, Honey. I'll be glad when you can tell me what's going on."

Fifteen minutes after Alen hung up with Joan, his phone rang. The call was from an unknown caller.

"Sheriff Arny," he answered.

"Sheriff, this is Detective Olsen with the CCPD. We met at the Colfax home."

"Yes, detective. How can I help you?"

"Could you come by the station, I'd like to chat with you?"

"Sure. Any particular time?"

"Now would be good."

"I'll be on my way then."

Alen was excited. Though he talked to Joan like he was working the case of George's death, he really just sat in his office, frustrated all day. He worked to release that frustration before returning home to Joan every evening. She assumed he wasn't telling her anything about the case, because he never talked to her about an ongoing investigation. He knew some officers and lawyers and probably judges too talked to their spouses about cases. But they really weren't supposed to. He was glad that was a rule he always followed. Because now he didn't have to explain to Joan that he didn't know anything. Nothing about the investigation. He would pass on his questions to his deputies. But the reality was, they had no jurisdiction in this case. If they were investigating and looking into his concerns, they weren't reporting back to him. He could have pulled rank, questioned them, leaned on them, and even yelled, releasing his frustration and possibly brow beating them into giving him info. But that's not who he was or how he worked. They were operating by the book and he had to suck it up, be patient and trust the process. Now he was excited because he thought that Detective Olsen reaching out to him meant they had solved the case and as a professional courtesy he was about to divulge the results of the investigation to him. Likely he had never been so wrong.

"Come on back Sheriff, let's have a chat," Detective Olsen said, and then he led Alen to an interrogation room.

"Whoa. Am I being questioned? I thought we were chatting."

"We are just chatting. You know how this works."

"Do I need an attorney?"

"I don't know. Did you do anything wrong?"

"No. Of course not."

"Then you shouldn't need an attorney. You aren't under arrest; I just have a few questions for you."

"Fine. Okay. How can I help?"

"First, can you tell me where you were the night George Colfax was murdered?"

"I was at home. With my wife. I went to work at my usual time on Wednesday morning. She is the only one who can collaborate my whereabouts."

"See how easy this is. You know the ropes and saved me three more questions. This shouldn't take any time at all."

"When did you borrow money from George? And when did you pay it back?"

"Honestly, I never borrowed money from George. I don't like mixing money and friendships. It never works out well."

"So, why did you say you say that at the Colfax home that day? And why did Marsha Colfax later say you already paid it back?"

"It's all I could think of at the moment, to not blurt out that the note said the mayor did it. I mean it didn't say what the mayor did, but I understand in that moment it would have been human nature to assume it meant the murder."

"Human nature for anyone but you?"

"No, of course I didn't mean that. But I am friends with the mayor, and I know he's not capable of murder."

"And why did Mrs. Colfax say you paid the loan back?"

"Actually, that I couldn't tell you. You would have to ask her that. Anything I could say here would be supposition and speculation."

"I see. Okay, fair enough."

"Sheriff, do you belong to any internet subscription sites?"

"I'm not sure I understand. What type of site are you asking about?"

"Do you belong to an internet group, club, or site that you pay to belong to?"

"Um, I pay for Google drive for cloud storage on a monthly basis. Is that what you mean?"

"No, sir. Do you belong to a club that maybe shares photos or videos?"

"I have a YouTube account where I watch videos and listen to music. Why?"

"Sheriff, let me be more clear."

"Please, Detective."

"Do you have a subscription to a porn site?"

"Gawd, no! Why would you ask that?"

"So, if we were to search your home and work computers, we would find no evidence of you visiting porn sites, or belonging to a porn site?"

"I'll give you access to my computers right now. My laptop is in my truck. But the answer is a definitive no."

"Just one more question. I understand the widow Colfax stayed at your house while hers was sealed. Did you witness anything unusual about her behavior? Did she confess or confide anything to you about her husband's murder?

"Confess? You think Marsha killed George?"

"That's not what I said. Please answer the question."

"Was her behavior unusual? For me, yes, it was. She is a very stoic and private woman. Most women would have been visibly shaken by the murder of their husband. Marsha didn't exhibit that behavior. So, for me it was odd, but for Marsha it was normal behavior. She didn't speak to me at all about George or his death. In fact, I hardly saw her. She stayed to herself. Maybe that's how she was dealing with her fear, grief, and anxiety."

"She was fearful? Of what? If she didn't talk to you, how would you know that?"

"Detective, if someone was killed in your home, while you were sleeping, would you not be afraid? Isn't that a normal human response to the situation?"

"So, you're speculating that she was fearful, based on your perception of typical human behavior?"

"Yes, I suppose I am."

"But you can't speculate as to why she said you paid your imaginary debt?"

"No, I can't. Is there anything else, detective? I'm late for dinner with my wife."

"Just one more question. When was the last time you saw the mayor?"

"Um, I'm not sure. My wife and I were scheduled to have dinner with Tim and Sophie last Friday night. But we cancelled. I suppose it's been a month or so since I saw him in person.

"Okay, that'll be all for now. Thanks for coming in."

"That's it? That's all? Do you know who killed George?"

"I can't discuss an..."

"Yeah, yeah, I know. Good night, Detective. I'll see myself out."

As soon as Alen returned to his car, he called Joan.

"Hi Sweetheart, I'm sorry, I'm running late. You won't believe this. I was just questioned by the detective in George's investigation. It was very weird."

"What? Are you kidding?"

"No, but I'm on the way home. I'll tell you all about it when I get there. How long until dinner's ready?"

"I made Spaghetti with coleslaw and green beans, But I haven't cooked the pasta until you get home, so it will hold until you're ready."

"Okay, on my way, I'll be there shortly."

There was someplace Alen wanted to stop on the way home. Now he knew he had time. He was sure Joan would forgive him for being a little longer than anticipated in getting home.

Chapter Ten

Alen entered through the garage door into the kitchen with one hand behind his back. He assumed Joan would be in the kitchen, but she wasn't which worked perfectly for him. He went to the sink, opened the cabinet underneath and pulled out a glass vase. He filled it with water, and understanding fully his limitations, removed the flowers from the clear cellophane sleeve and plopped them into the vase. He set them on the kitchen table in the center. Joan had already set the table for their dinner.

Then he said loudly, "Sweetheart, I'm home. Where are you?"

"On my way, Honey," she replied.

She walked into the kitchen carrying a two-arm sized load of sheets and towels on her way to the laundry room. She paused, puckered, and lifted her lips up to her husband for a kiss. He obliged and she continued to the laundry area.

"Let me start a load of the linens from the guest room. And I'll start dinner. But I can't wait for you to tell me what happened at the police station. I don't understand. Don't they know you and George were friends?"

"I've been thinking about it. The questions he asked were a little strange. I think it's precisely because we were friends that they questioned me. But I got to tell you, I'm even more perplexed about the case than I have been since the beginning."

He then told her about the interrogation.

"Honey, that's very odd. What do you think they were looking for? "

"I don't know. But I have a bad feeling. He asked if I subscribe to internet porn sites. "

"That's very odd. So, do you think George was involved in porn? Maybe that's what got him killed. Maybe Marsha found out he was surfing porn sites. But in my opinion, that's hardly reason to kill a man, but I understand it does really upset some people."

"I sure hope not. I can't imagine George being involved in anything that would degrade a living being. Unless it was a baby."

"No, no, no, Honey, it's too soon for that. That's not even funny."

"You're right, I'm sorry."

When she glanced over her shoulder at him sitting at the table, she noticed the flowers.

"Oh, Alen, thank you, Honey. They are beautiful!"

Alen was startled for a minute, looked up at his wife and followed where her eyes were looking. He spotted the flowers and remembered for the first time his surprise for her.

"You're welcome. Huh, in all this talk, I forgot I brought them to you. I hate this occupying all our time and focus. I can't wait until things get back to normal."

"When do you think you'll know what they are thinking?"

"When it's announced on the news. Just like everyone else."

There, it was out. No more hiding behind his frustration of not being involved, not being on the inside, not having his questions answered. Not knowing who killed his friend. But it did bring him around to another thought. His wife thought of it much faster than he did though, and voiced her concerns out loud.

"Alen, if George is dead, and the police suspected you were involved, I wonder if George's killer thinks you know something too...should we be worried? Are we in danger?"

"I don't know. I had the same thought. It's sobering and I don't like it."

"Should we leave town? Go on a trip? For the weekend maybe?"

"I don't want to run from our home in fear."

"Me either. But I would rather live to regret it, than to not."

"Let me think about it. Is that spaghetti done? I'm suddenly very hungry."

They ate together in companionable silence. While Alen was famished after removing himself from under the cloak of shame he felt he was under from not being forthcoming with Joan about his frustrations, Joan's appetite waned. She kept going over the pieces of this strange puzzle in her head.

There's Marsha's odd behavior, or lack of behavior. Pornography. What could porn sites have to do with it? How could they think Alen was involved? Could George be involved in porn? Is that what got him killed? And how did Jim, the mayor, come into the whole thing? Or did he? So, Jim is possibly a suspect in George's murder? Did Marsha know? Did she know about the porn, because obviously that came into the equation somehow? So, was Marsha the killer? Was I right to think there was a killer in my house? Or was it the mayor? Oh, gosh, I sure hope it's neither of them. Alen just lost his closest friend. If the mayor is involved, that will be another loss. Do we need to be worried? Are we in danger too?

"Okay, I've thought about it," Alen said startling Joan out of her dark and twisty thoughts.

"Good. Thought about what?" she answered.

"About going away for the weekend. I think we should do it. You're off tomorrow. I've been a persona non grata around my office for a week. We don't have anything keeping us from going somewhere. Where do you want to go?"

"Oh. Umm. I don't know. "

"Come on now, you said you wanted to start living life. You wanted to do new things in new places. Now's your chance."

"Well, I did think I would have time to think about it. You know, plan ahead."

"You?! Plan ahead? That's my line."

"I know, it seems we may have reversed roles. Is this some kind of Freaky Friday thing?"

"No. Today is Thursday. It would have to be a Tricky Thursday?"

"When do you want to go?"

"Tonight."

"Tonight? Seriously? Alen, are you becoming spontaneous on me?"

"Yes ma'am, I believe I am. I'll throw these dishes in the dishwasher. Go pack a bag."

"The linens are in the washer. If I leave them, they will mildew before we get back. But you know, I don't leave the dryer running when we aren't home. That's the number one cause of house fires."

"I'll put them in the dryer. By the time we get out of here they should be done. If they aren't, we'll risk it."

"Who are you and what have you done with my risk-averse husband?"

"I know. But it feels good. Right now, at this moment, I suddenly don't care about anything except spending time with you, and making sure you're safe."

"That detective didn't say anything about...'don't leave town' did he?"

Alen laughed, "No, he didn't. Quit looking for excuses and go pack a bag my beautiful bride."

"Where are we going?"

"I don't know yet."

"Then how do I know what to pack?"

"Jeans, casual clothes, hiking boots. It's just a weekend away. Nothing fancy." Alen already had an idea brewing. But he wanted to double-check the internet before he mentioned it. He put the linens in the dryer. Rinsed the dishes, loaded them in the dishwasher and then went to his office.

He was checking his idea on the internet, when he heard Joan coming down the stairs. At the bottom of the stairs she set her small rolling suitcase down and he heard the wheels rolling towards the kitchen.

"Done already?" he called from his office.

"Of course! You said pack, I packed."

"Did you pack for me too?"

"No. Are you going too?"

"Very funny, Mrs. Arny."

"Yes, I packed for you too. Are you ready to go?"

Still calling back and forth to each other, Joan in the kitchen and Alen in his office, he replied, "Just a minute. I have to call in and tell them I'm not coming to work tomorrow."

"Oh, yeah, that's a good idea," she muttered, tired of calling out across three rooms. She sat down at the kitchen table and thought for a moment to make sure she wasn't forgetting anything. She spotted the flowers. She carried the vase to the kitchen sink, pulled the flowers out, cut the stems and arranged them in the vase. Then she pulled four paper towels off the roll, wet them with water, and lifted the newly arranged flowers from the vase. She carefully wrapped the wet paper towels around the base of the stems. Then she wrapped the whole thing with plastic wrap and placed them back into the vase. She carried the vase back to the kitchen table.

Alen came walking into the kitchen and he strangely had a pep in his step and a smile on his face Joan had missed the last week.

"I know where we're going. Are you ready?"

He grabbed the suitcase and started towards the garage, she grabbed the vase and followed.

"Oh, good idea, you're bringing the flowers."

"You don't think I'm going to let them sit here alone and die, do you? The flowers go where I go. Speaking of which, where *are* we going?"

"It's a surprise."

"Mercy sakes, I hope you don't forget this one before we get there."

"Oh, aren't you a smarty pants, Mrs. Arny!"

Checking the gas gauge in Joan's SUV, he sighed. He drove to the nearest gas station and pulled up to a pump.

"How long a drive do we have ahead of us tonight?" Joan asked him.

"Not too long, but longer than a short drive. We shouldn't have to stop for gas again tonight if that's what you're asking."

"No, I was wondering if I should go in and buy drinks or snacks for the road."

"I'm still full from dinner. But we might want some dessert later. Drinks are never a bad idea. But I promise you'll get a good night's sleep because we're gonna need it."

She decided to let him have his fun and not badger him about where they were going. She would know soon enough and she was enjoying seeing him looking mischievous and happy again. She'd missed this side of him since George's death. She went inside and bought candy bars, bottles of water, and his favorite treat, a sports drink. Normally she would have brought bottles of water and trail mix from home, but in their haste to leave, she had not thought to pack snacks.

Alen headed north on I-37. Three hours later they pulled into a small town called Bandera.

Joan read the sign aloud, "Welcome to Bandera, population 877. Cowboy Capital of the World."

She laughed. "How can a place with only a population of 877 be the cowboy capital of the world?" she scoffed.

"Outside labor," Alen said dryly as he pulled up in front of a wood log cabin.

"I'll be right back; I'm going to check us in."

Joan waited patiently for him to return, but she was feeling a little bit giddy over the trip her husband managed to arrange so spontaneously. Though they hadn't talked about it since the night of the funeral, she realized, he really did hear her about wanting to do new things.

When he returned to the SUV, he said, "We're just staying here tonight. We'll check into our real destination tomorrow."

"Oh, and where is that?" she asked.

"We're gonna spend the weekend at a dude ranch!"

"Are you kidding?"

"Nope. Our first doing something new together."

Chapter Eleven

They slept in Friday morning after their late-night arrival. They checked out at 11:30 and went in search of food. After eating brunch, Alen drove them to the dude ranch that would be home for the next three days. They enjoyed being outside in the fall air, two trail rides a day, great home-cooked meals in the mess hall three times a day and visiting with other guests from all over the country there for the weekend ranching experience. There were no televisions. Cell phones worked, but were ignored. By Sunday afternoon, they were sore and ready to go home, but felt the most relaxed they had in years.

The thing that Joan had forgotten to pack was their cell phone chargers. She had a charger in the SUV, but they decided they didn't need and didn't want the phones, so they didn't worry about charging them through the whole weekend. When they left the dude ranch, Joan plugged in her phone to charge, because Alen said he wasn't ready to turn his back on yet.

"Thank you, Honey. This was a great weekend. It was fun, different. It felt like we were unplugged and living life. I'm getting what the memes are about now. Though, I guess if it was your job to ride hundreds of miles of fence and wrangle cattle it wouldn't feel that way. So, living life means doing something outside your work, even if you like what you do."

"Yep, I get it too."

"Wouldn't it be terrific if we could just go from one new experience to another."

"Sure. If we win the lottery, I suppose one could do that. Unfortunately, work has to happen for bills to be paid."

"I know. You know, I love reading books. But I always wonder about those characters who can fly off on some whim and never worry about money. But you know, there are more and more people who are moving abroad. There's a thing now, it's called digital nomads. It's people who work online and don't have to go to an office, so they can work from anywhere. Maybe we could be digital nomads."

"Okay. See if you can find us jobs and we'll talk more about it. But where would you want to live?"

"I don't know. Maybe nowhere for a while. Maybe a new place every month or every three months."

Alen knew Joan wouldn't be able to find jobs for them where they could travel the world. So, he worked to quell the anxieties that naturally arose for him from thinking about a life that unstructured. And he turned on the radio.

Fifteen miles from home, Joan remembered they left the dryer running when they left town Thursday night.

"Oh, Alen, I hope our house is still standing. If it burned down, no one would have been able to reach us all weekend."

They were both shocked speechless when Alen replied, "Que sera sera."

Joan started thinking about what she would really miss if it was all gone. And Alen did too. Their sweet dog was already long gone. They both realized, there wasn't much there that they would miss. At least not much that couldn't be replaced.

Joan had her mother's collection of cookie jars. But she mostly had them because she had them. She pulled them down from the space above the kitchen cabinets twice a year and washed them. But they didn't bring her joy. She had a collection of frogs. They brought her joy and made her smile. But if they were gone forever, she realized, she would still be Joan.

Alen pulled into the driveway and into the garage.

"Well, it's still standing and doesn't look any worse for wear."

"Darn, I was kinda starting to think about how much we could travel with the insurance money."

"Joan!"

"I know! I'm appalled at myself for the thought. I don't know where this acute wanderlust is coming from, but it's getting kind of serious. I wonder if it can be treated medically."

"Maybe you should research that too."

"Just leave the suitcase here in the laundry room. I'll take the toiletries up after dinner and put the clothes into wash. I bet they're pretty stinky."

"Do you want to take a shower?"

"Yeah, I really do, I feel dusty."

"Why don't you go up and get one first, then. I can wait a bit until dinner."

"Okay, I'll make it quick."

"No rush, Sweetheart."

When Joan came back downstairs, the washer was already running and Alen was plating left over Spaghetti for their dinner.

"Honey! You didn't have to cook."

"I know. But I also know you are tired and have to go back to work tomorrow."

"You too."

"Yeah, but these days I'm not working as hard as you are."

Dinner was quiet. They were both thinking.

After dinner, Alen did the dishes while Joan checked her email. Then he went up to take a shower. She didn't know why it felt like she needed to sneak, or that she was sneaking around, but as soon as he cleared the third step she did an internet search for 'digital nomad jobs'.

Monday morning, they were back into their normal routine. Except Alen turned on the television to catch the morning news. He was beginning to feel really out of the loop after three days away. He imagined half the city would be in chaos because of it. He knew that wouldn't be true, it felt uncomfortable to not know what had happened in three days in the city.

Joan left for work as usual, but Alen poured himself another cup of coffee and sat down in the great room to watch the morning news with more attention. He was feeling a bit sorry for himself. The weekend had been great. And this morning he really didn't want to go back to work and sit in his office.

Joan has wanderlust and I have anti-cubicle syndrome. For the first time in my life I don't want to go to work. I don't want to sit behind my desk, but I might as well get my butt to work, he thought. He stood up watched as the morning news was ending before reaching for the remote when the daytime programming started. Just as he pushed the button, he heard the music and saw the Breaking News banner flash before the TV shut off. He wasn't sure why, but it was important for him to see the breaking news. He pushed the power button again and waited what seemed an interminable amount of time before the set returned to life.

We are awaiting a news conference with a spokesman from the police department scheduled to start any moment. Recapping, we are told arrests took place this morning in the Councilman Colfax murder investigation. All we know at this time is there were multiple suspects arrested, we are waiting for the briefing to begin. We have an unofficial report from sources inside the investigation that some type of crime syndicate has also been infiltrated. There are the police captain and the public information officer approaching the microphone now. Let's listen.

Alen didn't sink back into his recliner. He paced and watched the screen intently waiting. *Multiple arrests? A crime syndicate? What in the world had George gotten himself into and why didn't he let me know if he needed help?* he thought.

"I'm Mike Nickels, the Corpus Christi Police Department Information Officer. I have a brief statement to read and the Captain is here to answer a few questions when I'm done.

Early this morning in a multi-agency operation multiple arrests were conducted simultaneously throughout Nueces County. These arrests were a result of an eighteen-month undercover investigation."

Eighteen months? George was just killed two weeks ago. How could this investigation lasted eighteen months? Alen wondered.

"Arrested for Sexual Abuse of minors, Sexual exploitation of minors, possession and distribution of child porn and possession of methamphetamines are five individuals operating a website for the purpose of creating and distributing pornography depicting sexual abuse of minors. They are Wiley Pratt, Charles Reynolds, Walker Tyrell, Richard Warwick, and Quintin D'Angelo.

Child pornography? George? George doesn't even like children. No way. What does this have to do with George?

With the added charge of capital murder for the death of City Councilman George Colfax, is one Noah Parsons.

Capital murder? That means he was either in the process of the commission of a crime, like maybe he was planning to rob the house and then killed George. Or it was murder for hire? Who would want George dead bad enough to put out a contract on him? And why? Alen found that he had even more questions, now that the case was supposedly solved.

"Additionally, Mayor Jim Ellis was arrested and charged with possession and distribution of child porn, international kidnapping, and obstruction of justice."

What? Jim is involved? International kidnapping? Wait- this has got to a nightmare! I've got to go see what this is all about. Hopefully Detective Olsen will talk to me now that the arrests are made.

Alen went to the kitchen, picked up his keys and headed for the garage and his truck. He had to get to the bottom of this. His phone rang. It was Joan. He pressed the button on his steering wheel that routed the call through his radio for hands free communication.

"Honey, have you heard the news?"

"Yes, I just watched the news brief. I hadn't left home yet. I don't understand. I don't understand any of this. I'm headed to the police station to try to talk to Detective Olsen. I need more details."

"Okay. I understand. It's confusing to me too. I wonder if they told Marsha anything?"

"Oh, I didn't think of Marsha. I'll ask Detective Olsen if she found out like we did through the TV news, or if they clued her in already. I still can't figure out what any of this has to do with George. When I leave there, I'll check on her. But yeah, I guess all our concerns about her were unfounded."

Alen walked into the station and approached the desk.

"I'm Sheriff Alen Arny. I need to speak to Detective Olsen, please."

"Just a moment, please," the officer responded as he picked up the receiver for the desk phone, dialed a number and waited a brief moment.

"Detective, the sheriff is here and asking to see you. Yes, okay."

"Sheriff, the detective will see you now. Do you know your way?"

"Yes, I've been here before. Thank you."

Alen took the elevator and wound his way through the roomful of desks to Detective Olsen's desk. The detective stood and reached out a hand to shake Alen's hand.

"I was planning to call you but it's been crazy. Have a seat."

"Will you tell me what's going on? Can you break this down and explain it to me? I saw the news brief and to be honest, it makes no sense at all to me. How have you been investigating a two-week-old murder for eighteen months?"

"Let's sit down. Now that the arrests have been made, and because you are also a victim, I can tell you what you need to know."

"I'm a victim? How am I a victim? Just last week you were questioning me as if I was guilty of a crime."

"Yeah, I'm sorry about that but at that time we still weren't certain who was who in this whole mess. Would you like to call Mrs. Arny to come and hear all this too?"

"Um. Well, she's at work. Does this somehow have something to do with her too?"

"Actually, it does. But it's up to you. I thought she might have questions too."

"Of course. But she doesn't answer her cell phone while she's on duty. She usually calls me on her break, but that's not for another couple of hours." Alen was visibly confused. If he thought the press conference was bewildering, and the thought that somehow, he was a victim disconcerting, the thought that Joan was involved in this too was downright perplexing.

"That's okay, I can call over to Metrocom and they can send her over here. It won't take long." The detective picked up his phone, connected to an operator, told her what he needed, and then waited silently for a moment.

"Yes, this is Detective Olsen at PD. Could you please ask your dispatcher Joan Arny to come over to the PD? I need to speak with her. Thank you."

He then turned to Alen, "While we wait, can I get you a bottle of water, cup of coffee, or something?"

"Um, no thanks. For probably the first time in my life, I think I've had enough coffee for the moment."

Alen's phone rang. It was Joan.

"Honey, are you still at the police station?"

"Yes, I'm here. We're waiting for you."

"Well, since you answered your phone, I assume they haven't arrested you. What's going on?"

"I don't know yet. Detective Olsen says that I'm a victim in this case. And it involves you too. But it doesn't make any sense. We are waiting until you get here and then the fine detective assures me he will explain everything."

"I'm on my way, I'll be there in a couple of minutes. Don't start without me."

"We won't," he answered as the phone line went dead.

When Joan arrived, the detective said, "Why don't we move to the conference room. It will be more comfortable and private."

"Well, at least he didn't say interrogation or interview room, right, Honey?"

"Yeah, I've already visited one of those. I wouldn't call them comfortable," he answered softly as he followed Joan, following the detective down a corridor.

Olsen opened a door to a carpeted room with a table that would seat ten people, the walls were painted a soothing shade of silvery grey. The chairs were executive rolling chairs with high backs. Alen noted that in comparison to the interview room he sat in last week, this room seemed luxurious. Almost like a corporate conference room. They each sat in a chair and Detective Olsen began to explain.

"We've been investigating an internet child pornography ring for eighteen months to determine who was backing it, where the children were coming from, and other aspects of the group."

"What does that have to do with George? I can't believe he was part of that," Alen asked.

"Councilman Colfax was not part of the organization. He was, however, a subscriber to the VIP level of the site. That is what ultimately led to his murder."

"Why? Why would they kill a subscriber?"

"Well, apparently in this case, Councilman Colfax was the one doing the threatening. These sites are very expensive, apparently the councilman actually belonged to several of them. His personal finances are in ruins. When he couldn't pay his subscription fees anymore, he threatened to go to the authorities, and the guys who run this thing decided they couldn't have that. So, they put a contract out on him. They hired Noah Parsons to kill him."

"And the Mayor is involved in this thing too? The news said International kidnapping? Seriously? Our mayor? Jim Ellis?" Alen asked.

"From our investigation, we believe the Mayor is who introduced the councilman to the site."

"He also was a subscriber to the site? He wasn't part of the organization?" Joan asked.

"Well, it started out that way. This was a very specialized website. It featured photos and videos of not just children, not just sexual acts with children, but violent sexual abuse of children."

"Oh my gosh, you mean like the rape of children?" Joan gasped.

"Yes, and worse. Anyway, you had to pay for your subscription with cryptocurrency which is why it took so long for us to track down all the players. Or you could earn points by uploading, supplying the pictures and videos to the site. That is how the Mayor was funding his addiction. He was kidnapping children from Mexico and providing them to this porn ring. We have evidence of as many as twenty children he provided to these sick people."

"I can assure you we knew nothing of this! We would never participate in something this barbaric, let alone illegal. We love children. How or why could you think we are involved?" Joan asked.

"What? You had investigators undercover in this ring, and they stood by and watched children being abused?" Alen's voice was rising more than he wanted it to. He was normally calm in a crisis, but this was just too much. He was envisioning things he never wanted to see.

"They couldn't blow their cover."

"And Marsha? Is Marsha Colfax involved in this in any way?" Alen asked.

"We can't find any evidence that she was involved at all. Other than the fact that the note she gave you on the day of the murder, the one that said the Mayor did it...was in her handwriting, not the councilman's."

"Detective, you said I was a victim. I don't understand. I'm not a child. I'm not involved. How could I be a victim?"

"Because, Councilman Colfax's user ID and password for the site where your initials and date of birth."

"So, she knew. All along. She knew that both George and the Mayor were involved in this unimaginable depravity?" Joan wailed.

"We think so. At least at some point she became aware. But like I said, there is no evidence that she was anything more than a victim, like the two of you."

"Okay, let's just get this straight...worst case scenario, my best friend George was willing to cast suspicion on me, frame me for his perversion. Yeah, that could have ended badly for me. But in relation to what was going on here...I do not consider myself a victim. Those children are the victims. Their parents are victims. But not me. And not Mrs. Colfax either. How can she be considered a victim?"

"She lost her husband to murder. That makes her a victim."

"I'm sorry, but in this case, I think it makes her lucky," Joan answered.

"Yes ma'am. I understand your sentiments," Detective Olsen stated.

"Do you have photos of the men arrested? I hate to admit this, but Marsha Colfax seemed so unaffected by George's death, when she was staying with us, while she was locked out of her house, I followed her one day. She met a man in a café. I wonder who he is and if he was part of this."

"I do have photos. But we were also following Mrs. Colfax. The man you saw was the loan officer for their mortgage. We questioned him. They are in arrears and were facing foreclosure on the home. Mrs. Colfax is waiting on the life insurance money to catch up the mortgage payments. She was meeting him to ask for another extension before foreclosure proceeding would start."

"Well, honestly, if I found out my husband was a depraved sicko and I was going to lose my home, I guess I might not be too sad about his death either."

"Indeed," the detective responded.

"Is there anything else you need to tell us or are we free to go? I have an overwhelming need for a shower." Alen asked.

"No Sheriff. You're free to go. Thank you for your cooperation in this case."

"Joan, let's go home."

Chapter Twelve

Joan arrived home first. She pulled her SUV into the garage and left the garage door open for Alen to pull in as well. She walked around to the back of her car and leaned against the back bumper to wait for Alen.

For some reason, she was feeling claustrophobic. She didn't want to go into the house. The day was overcast and there was a nice breeze blowing. The late October day actually felt cool and she enjoyed the breeze. She assumed Alen got stopped by a red light that she didn't and would be home any minute. But after more time passed, she wondered if he stopped somewhere or just got caught at every traffic light between the police station and home. If he was called to a crime scene or something, she felt sure he would have called. Then she remembered that her phone was still on silent in her purse from work. She reached into her purse, pulled out the phone and looked at it. There were no missed calls from Alen or anyone else. She turned up the volume and waited. Then she recalled when she spoke to him that morning when he was on the way to the police station to try to get answers, that he said he would check on Marsha when he left there. She didn't think he would stop at Marsha's without letting her know. But even if he did, she couldn't bring herself to go into the house. She continued to lean against the SUV and wait. She was desperately trying not to form visions in her mind about what they learned at the police station about their friends. Even the words were too horrific to want to contemplate without any images to accompany them.

She realized what she needed and she looked up to see Alen's truck approaching. She waited for him to pull into the garage, and then she walked in to the passenger side door and tapped on the window.

"Hiya, stranger. Did you get stopped at every single red light? I've been waiting for hours."

"Ha-ha, yes, a few red lights, but I stopped at Mac's and got us ice cream bars. Like the Golden Girls, this day requires ice cream." He reached into the bag and produced her favorite chocolate covered vanilla ice cream bar, stretching across the seat to hand it out the passenger side window to her.

"How come you're waiting out here?"

"I don't know why; I can't seem to face going into the house. I feel like somehow it shrunk and I won't fit in there or something. It's quite strange actually. I was wondering if you might like to go somewhere to walk. An open space."

"You want to go to the beach?"

"No. At the moment, tan sand and an empty beach feels dead and depressing. Maybe because of the clouds. I want to go someplace green. Some place that is so obviously alive, that I can't feel disconnected from life, like I'm feeling right now. What about a trail walk at Blucher Park?"

"That sounds great, Sweetheart. Do you want to go in the truck or yours?"

"Just stay where you are," she said as she opened the door they were talking through, hoisted her purse into the floor, not letting go of her ice cream, and climbed into the truck.

"I think I'm almost out of gas, anyway."

They walked through the park, holding hands, each in thought. Each trying to digest the vitriol of the information they learned today around and past the lumps in their throats.

Joan spoke first, "Oh, I forgot to ask if you wanted to go check on Marsha before we came here."

"No. No, I don't. At the moment, I feel she's just as guilty as I am. I don't have any sympathy for her, and I don't want to be around her."

"What do you mean as guilty as you are? How are you guilty of anything? This has nothing to do with you."

"But it does. Don't you see. I'm supposed to be an enforcer of the law. I'm supposed to be able to read people. And here, my best friend and a close friend were involved in something this heinous and I had no clue. No idea. What kind of law enforcement officer does that make me? Beyond incompetent?"

"Alen, I don't care who you are. You can't know everything about everyone. Sure, we feel we know people. We feel we know what people are capable of, but we don't really. Especially people who are capable of crimes, they are masters at hiding. You know this. How in the world can you think any of this is a reflection on you? I read a thing on the internet that you are likely to walk past 36 murderers in your life. I know several people who know someone that killed someone and they never knew the person was capable of it."

"But Joan, it's my job. And I wonder if this isn't worse than murder. I mean these poor children have to live with the fear, the trauma, the memories. Isn't that worse than death? At least for the children, maybe not the parents. I feel nasty and dirty for even knowing someone involved in this stuff. And George? George spent his whole adult life openly not liking children."

"Maybe this is why. Maybe he didn't trust himself to be around them. Maybe looking at those pictures stopped him from being a pedophile. We'll never know. But at least he never actually caused the harm to any of them?"

"Really? You think so? If there were no sick people out there paying to see those pictures, there wouldn't be so many functioning websites charging for them for George to lose his house! I've got to tell you, Sweetheart, I think it's time for me to resign my position."

"Alen, you just turned in your intention to run for re-election."

"I know. But this city deserves someone better than me."

"You are hurting right now. This is not the best time to make a life decision."

"When is? A week from now, a month, a decade?"

Just then, as they were walking through an area of particularly thick vegetation, at the same time, something light and out of character in their peripheral vision caught their attention. It was a used condom hanging on a low-lying shrub like a Christmas ornament on a tree.

"Yeah. I don't think I can do this anymore. Things are changing, Joan. They are changing too fast. Even if I didn't feel my intuition was totally off, do I want to be part of a system where our leaders are so depraved?"

"But you are one of the good guys. Are you just going to leave it all to them? Shouldn't you stay to try to fight the corruption?"

"No, I don't think so."

"Okay, then. What will you do?"

"I don't know. I suppose I have to find something to do. Something to make money. I'm too young to retire, and even if I did retire, what would I do all day?"

"Well, if you are serious about doing something else, I've actually been researching and might have an idea."

"Oh, yeah, what's that?"

Without realizing it, they were both walking back towards the car. The obscene offensive "decoration" had spoiled the nature walk for them both.

"Remember after George's funeral, we talked about a bucket list."

"Yeah, I remember. You said you wanted to do new things. I took you to a dude ranch. That was new."

"It was. And it was a great weekend. I can't believe we just got back yesterday. It seems a world and a lifetime away."

"You want to move to a dude ranch? That's a lot of hard work. I suspect after much more than a couple of weeks or a month at the most it would be pretty tedious and boring too."

"No, I don't want to move to a dude ranch, silly. But you do bring up an excellent point. Visiting somewhere for a few weeks or a month seems ideal, doesn't it? There isn't enough time to get bored, or caught up in local politics."

"Yeah, but we can't just travel all the time."

"Why not? We don't have children or grandchildren to tether us to a place. We don't have pets that would make it hard to travel. Why can't we hop and skip from one beautiful place to another?"

"Joan, Sweetheart. Did we win the lottery and you didn't tell me?"

They were back to the truck and they got inside.

Alen veered off topic for a minute. "Are you hungry?"

"Yes, actually I am."

"Let's go to Frank's."

"Okay, that sounds good."

Alen drove, and Joan went back to the topic of the discussion.

"No, we didn't win the lottery. But I did find out some interesting things. Did you know that there are people all over the world who have someone come into their home to house sit and take care of their pets while they travel?"

"Really? Isn't that kind of creepy? And risky, letting strangers stay in your house? Who would do that?"

"Thousands of people do. There are services that you sign up with, and they vet you, through background checks and references. There is a House Sitters magazine and a House Sitters Academy, that will train you in what you need to know. Home and pet owners post listings on the sites for the dates they need someone to stay in their home. There are people who travel all over the world and do this all the time. They might have a two-week house sit in Cairo and then a month in Mexico. Doesn't it sound like fun?"

"Do the sitters get paid to do this?"

"No. The service is free. In exchange you have a free place to stay in all these locations."

"So, how do people afford to do this? International travel is expensive."

They were pulling into the parking lot of Frank's Italian Restaurant, where they had date night a little over a week before. They both marveled at how much their world had changed since that dinner. Again, they paused the discussion while they went in and were seated promptly, due to being one of the first early diners to arrive.

This time when the hostess seated them, it was Joan who spoke up.

"Hi, we are starving and we're ready to order as soon as a waiter can get to us."

"Okay, if you like, I'll be happy to take your order and pass it on to your waiter."

Again, it was Joan who spoke up this time.

"Thank you, we'll have two spaghettis and a bottle of the house red with two glasses of water, please."

"Yes, ma'am, I'll turn this in for you now, and your waiter will be here with your drinks shortly."

"Thanks," Alen and Joan said in unison.

"Spaghetti for you too tonight? Not your regular?"

"No. Spaghetti is the ultimate comfort food and I think we both need comforting tonight. Now back to this idea. I've been thinking about it. So, most people who decide to do this full time, sell their house, and all their belonging, in a big estate type sale. You only need to keep what you are going to travel with, so basically you only need what will fit in two suitcases, each."

"You mean sell everything?"

"Yeah. They say it's very liberating."

"Your mother's cookie jar collection?"

"Especially my mother's cookie jar collection. They are just grease and dust magnets. So anyway, you have your military retirement income. In two years, you can file for early retirement and start getting your Social Security benefits. Two years after that I can file. With no house payment, no car payment, and our only expenses being food, plane tickets, and sightseeing, I figured out, we can easily do it on the proceeds of selling everything until we can start bumping our income up when we file for Social Security."

"You're serious about this!"

"Yeah. I am. Why not?"

"Sell everything? How do we even know this will work? What if we don't have a place to house sit?"

"Yes, sell everything."

The waiter came and poured their wine. They stopped talking while he was there. He left discreetly and quickly aware he was interrupting a conversation.

"If we have a few days, or a week between house sits we stay in a hotel. Alen, can we seriously consider this? I mean, if you're going to resign anyway?"

"What about you? Are you ready to retire?"

"Alen, I've been a 911 dispatcher for twenty-five years. I answer on average almost 100 emergency calls every day that I work. As a department we answer 50,000 calls a month, for 600,000 calls a year. That's why I didn't even recognize Marsha's voice, or her address when I answered the call the day George died. I'm on auto pilot. I deal with a lot of tragedy, anguish, fear, devastation. Yes. I'm ready to leave all that behind. I want to not have to care about anything except what to cook for dinner, to love on a dog. Even if it isn't mine. This is a way we can have pets in our lives, without becoming so attached that it's heartbreaking when it's their time to go. We know up front that each pet will only be ours for a little while. But we still get to come home to wagging tails and puppy kisses. We still get to curl up next to or hold a dog on a cold night."

She stopped again when the waiter brought their salads and again made a hasty exit.

Joan chuckled... "I wonder if he thinks we're fighting?"

"No way. See these eyes?" Alen pointed to his eyes with the tines of his fork to make his point. "These eyes are looking at you in a way that no one could mistake as anger."

"Hmm, what are those eyes saying?" she asked.

"These eyes are saying, how did I get so lucky to find a beautiful, intelligent, adventurous, woman willing to marry this bald incompetent coot?"

"Alen Arny! You are not incompetent! And self-deprecation is not attractive on you, not even one little bit. But you are a lucky man, no doubt. I married a strong, brave, self-confident man, and that's who I want to spend my life with exploring this great big beautiful globe."

The waiter came bringing two plates heaping with spaghetti and removed their salad plates.

"Are you saying we can do this?" Joan asked as she twirled spaghetti around the end of her fork, and then took a healthy bite of the soul comforting Italian sauce and pasta.

"No. I'm saying I still have a lot of questions. I want to put pen and paper to the numbers. You've obviously had time to think about this and have your questions answered. I need that too." Then he took his first bite of spaghetti.

They ate in silence, neither one having eaten since breakfast. And they thought...since talking wasn't conducive to the shoveling in of the cuisine that would abate their appetites.

"You know, I get the whole cookie jar thing. But I'm pretty sure you have an entire suitcase full of those crazy socks you like to wear. Does that mean you'll be running around wearing only socks? Or are you willing to part with them for this wild adventure?"

"Honey, a wild adventure is living in the Australian outback with a guy named Crocodile Dundee. I'm just asking you to move from one house, one country to another every month or so."

"But I hate moving."

"But it's not like we're loading up the truck like the Clampetts and moving across town or across country. All we'll have to move is a couple of suitcases. No breakable lamps, no shedding houseplants. I have to admit, I'm already starting to feel the liberation of shedding all our worldly goods."

"You mean all the stuff that's been so important to us for years, decades, a lifetime?"

"I'm sure it's going to be hard to do. I'm not promising to not get emotional about it from time to time. But I think the experiences, the places we'll see, the people we'll meet will be worth it."

The waiter approached again. "Can I interest you in dessert?"

"I'm interested, but I'll be enjoying dessert at home this evening. Check please," Alen answered.

Joan smiled. And after the check was paid, they walked out of the restaurant, hand in hand, shoulder touching shoulder, to Alen's truck.

"When we get home, will you show me some of these websites you've been reading, so I can see for myself how this might all work?"

"Sure, Honey. Anything you need." And she did.

The next morning, Joan and Alen left home at the same time going to work. But their days would end very differently.

Chapter Thirteen

Joan went to work as usual. She spent her day assisting people in need. She was the calm voice to help them in time of crisis. A skill she perfected over the years. But this job wasn't like any other job. On one hand, one needed to become hardened to the human tragedy of it all. Her days routinely included death and devastation. Some days, she skated through with more minor issues, but all day, every day, she dealt with sadness, shock, disbelief, grief, from the people on the other end of the communication line. On the other hand, more and more lately, she also had a front-row or at least a second-row seat to the changing times, to the depravity, to the loss of respect for human life. Indeed, all beings. She was beginning to feel herself weaken. The calls she was taking were affecting her more. Maybe because instead of the calls being about accidents and the natural course of life and death, the calls increasingly highlighted the atrocities that human beings were capable of doing to one another.

On this day, like he did each day since George's murder, Alen drove to the sheriff's office, fixed himself a cup of coffee, went to his office and closed the door. He heard a soft quite knock on the door.

"Come in," he answered while he booted up his computer. A young deputy came in.

"I'm sorry to bother you, sir. These requisitions came in yesterday while you were out and need signatures. Also, I'm to remind you the budget is due next week."

"Fine, fine. Leave them there. I'll sign them, and yes, I'll give the budget some thought."

"Yes, sir," the deputy said, laying the paperwork on the nearest corner of Alen's desk and he gingerly backed out the door closing it on his way.

Alen never gave the requisitions another thought. He pulled up the internet and set out to read all he could find about international house and pet sitting. His first thought was that it was a crazy idea, and his second was it was a brilliant idea. Once he felt he understood how the process worked of securing these house-sitting positions, he began pulling up flight information and prices. He needed some more realistic ideas, so he signed up for a couple of the house sitter sites that had a free trial. He browsed the listings for available opportunities and started filling out an imaginary calendar.

Once he had a few months of potential sits mapped out, he went back to the travel site to see what it would cost to fly from each of the points to the next point. He tried to find the most extreme travel options for the worst-case scenario in terms of cost.

His imaginary hypothetical situation had him traveling from Texas to China, from China, to a Caribbean island, from there to Australia, to Europe and on to the Ukraine. With those costs in hand, he then went to a website that listed cost of living for cities all over the world. It listed everything from the cost of groceries and produce, a cappuccino in a restaurant, eating out, taxi or bus fares, and for each of the locations he made what he felt was a reasonable budget of expenses in each location.

He was annoyed when his phone rang, just as he was about to add up all of his numbers. But he looked at the phone, contemplating ignoring the call, but saw it was Joan. His anxiety level rose as he answered it.

"Hello, Sweetheart. I have to tell you, these middle of your shift calls are making my really nervous. They mean something bad has happened."

"Honey, it's my lunch break. I usually call you on my lunch break."

"It's lunch time? Really? Wow, the morning flew by."

"What's kept you so preoccupied?"

"Uh, well, actually, I was looking into this wacky idea of yours."

"Alen Arny, I am your wife, I am above average intelligence, I am a productive and respected member of society and I do not have wacky ideas." Though her tone was stern, she was secretly delighted. She knew exactly what "wacky" idea her husband was referring to, and the idea that he was giving it a thought was exciting, the thought that it stole his morning away without him realizing it was confirmation that it was at least a little bit exciting to him too.

"Yes, dear. I should have said, that idea you had that sounded wacky and is possibly proving to be a genius idea."

"Wow, genius? We went from wacky to genius in the space of a few seconds!"

"Not exactly. I tossed and turned last night thinking about it and this morning I've been reading and studying and planning, not a few seconds."

"I'm excited you're even giving it a thought. What have you come up with?"

"Well, it actually looks possible. And doable. And it makes sense. How long do you think it would take us to be ready to go?"

"Seriously?"

"Yes, seriously."

"I'm ready now."

"I get that, Sweetheart, but I mean really ready. Like we have to sell the house and all the stuffs. What else?"

"Hmm, well, I need to renew my passport, I think that takes a few weeks but you can pay a little extra and expedite it if you have pending travel. You've kept yours up to date. Depending on where you are house sitting, some countries require a visa before you travel, others give you an automatic travel visa when you arrive."

"Yeah, yeah, I know, so we only pick house sits at first where we can just go without the visa hassle."

"As far as selling everything we can handle it all our selves, with selling online and/or yard sales, or we can hire an auction or estate company to handle it for us. Then the time it takes to do whatever we need to do to the house to sell it. I honestly don't know how to tell you exactly how long it will take."

"Well, if I was working on it full time, it would speed things up, right?"

"Sure, but..."

"I'm going to get some lunch and start a plan of action. We can talk about it tonight when we get home. Okay?"

"Okay," she answered a bit perplexed at his fast decision and turn around, but the butterflies of excitement began to flutter in her gut.

"I love you, Sweetheart, thank you for coming up with this idea."

"I love you too, Honey. I'll see you at home and I'm looking forward to what you've come up with."

They hung up, and Alen realized his mind was already made up. He was feeling a buzz of excitement he had not felt in some time. He went out and got a sandwich for lunch, made a few phone calls and started making a checklist."

Joan always got home before Alen. But not this day. She was surprised to open the garage door and see his truck there. When she opened the door from the garage into the kitchen, there sat her husband at the kitchen table, with his laptop and a notebook, working on a list.

"Hi there, it's kind of fun to come in and you be here. What's up?"

"Joan, Sweetheart, I sure hope you'll forgive me."

"Forgive you for what?"

"Well, I don't usually make major life decisions without discussing them with you first. And this affects you too. But I just couldn't help myself. I didn't want to interrupt you at work. This whole mess with George has already cost you time off."

"Honey, what on earth? It's okay whatever it is. Just talk to me," she said as she set her purse down and sat down at the table with her husband.

"I realized I'm really suffering a crisis of faith. In myself. I realize I can't trust my instinct about people. I look at strangers and I wonder what they've done. Intellectually I know that the world is full of good and decent people, but right now, I see monsters everywhere. As such, I am no longer effective or good for this city or the department."

"Okay. I understand. I've been realizing how my job has changed over the years and how the calls I answer have migrated from being sad to incomprehensible. So, I'm guessing, you want to pull your petition for re-election? It's okay, if that's what you need. I'm behind you."

"No."

"No? You want to resign now?"

"No. I'm sorry. I already did."

"Oh. Okay. I didn't really see that coming, but I'm not totally surprised either."

"So, for a while your income and my military pension is what we have coming in."

"No problem. We can tighten our belts."

"It won't be for long, I don't think."

"Yeah? You have something in mind you want to do?"

"I do. I want to become a house and pet sitter. I love the idea of having a pet again without the emotional investment of knowing I'll likely outlive them. I like the idea of seeing new places, having new experiences, and traveling the world with my one true love."

"OOhhhhh, you really know how to butter a girl up!"

"Are you sure this is something you want to do? I know you were just researching it and thinking about. I realized after I resigned that I never asked if you were sure you wanted to do it."

"Yes. I do. I want to have fun before I'm, well, we're too old to enjoy it. I've also read traveling keeps you young. It's way better than sitting in a recliner watching television all day."

"Great. I started making lists and planning, but we do need to make some decisions."

And that's how Alen and Joan's days ended differently. Alen no longer had a job, and Joan was now the couple's major breadwinner.

"I'll start dinner, and you can tell me what's on your list."

"Oh, instead of regular dinner, would you just make Texas Caviar and your Chocolate Pie?"

"Um, yeah, sure, why not? Anything but spaghetti."

"Since tomorrow is your day off, I took the liberty to schedule some people to come to the house."

"Oh, who is that?"

"I have two realtors coming in the morning, two auction companies and two estate sale companies later in the day. I figure that will give us an idea of how much we want to do ourselves and hopefully, if we want to hire someone, we can choose from those who come tomorrow. I know we can't know how long it will take to sell the house. And how to choose a date to sell all the furniture if we don't know when the house will sell. But I would like to get on with this as soon as possible. Wouldn't it be great if we could spend Christmas someplace cold and snowy?"

"Well, yeah, it would, but Alen, if you are talking about this Christmas, that's only two months away!"

"I know. I'm just thinking, Christmas here in Corpus is going to be so depressing. George is gone. Jim's in jail. I don't know who I trust. Whose Christmas party will we go to? I think it would be better if we are traveling. So, my worst-case idea is...if we have to, we can use some of our savings to do a housesit somewhere over the holidays, even if we have to come back here. Heck, even if it's someplace in the U.S."

"I like the way you think. Maybe we could ease into it."

"I can't tell you how excited I am to get away from a life full of crime and drama!"

"Yeah, me too. Do you think we'll be bored?"

"Not for a minute!"
The Universe had other ideas for Alen and Joan.

Chapter Fourteen

The following day, after meeting with two real estate agents and four different possible companies to charge with selling all their worldly possessions they sat down to make decisions.

If they wanted to be done with it all super-fast, they could hire one of the auction companies. In two days, they would sell the house, the contents, and even their vehicles, if they wanted. And it was likely everything would sell at least for some price, with nothing to disburse with after the sale. But the down side was they would have no control over the selling price. With the estate sale companies, they could have a little more control over the prices with the company's expertise as guidance, but there was a risk of things not selling. Using a real estate agent for the house would assure them the most control over who bought the house and for how much. But could also potentially take weeks or months, or even years.

One auction company had an available date the end of November and one estate sale company had an available date in early December. The other two companies didn't have available dates until after the new year.

But if they scheduled a sale date and all the contents sold before the house sold, where would they live while they waited for the house to sell? And the real estate agents advised them that the house would sell better furnished than empty.

They were hard decisions to make. Even scary a little bit.

But over the weekend, Joan wrestled with going back to work on Monday. The thought of never having to deal with another phone call that someone was losing a loved one, or someone was mistreating an animal, or another mass shooting, was so appealing that she discovered she was downright jealous that Alen wouldn't be going to his job on Monday. Suddenly, she just wanted it to all be over with.

They looked at the finances again and all the hypothetical costs scenarios Alen mapped out. It was possible that they could be house sitters for a year on their savings, barring any catastrophic events, if the house didn't sell. So, they opted to list the house with a real estate agent, and they booked the auction company for the last week in November. They had three and a half weeks until their current life would begin dismantling.

As it turned out, they worried for no reason. The house sold in two weeks to anxious buyers who wanted to take possession the first of December to get settled into their new home before Christmas.

They notified the auction house to add their vehicles to the list of auction items, and they prepared to leave the house the day before the auction and move into a hotel until they could arrange their first house sit gig. Joan gave her two-week notice.

Alen told Joan to start looking for a house sit someplace cold for Christmas. They would be ready to leave Corpus Christi and all its tragedy behind and begin a new life, a new adventure, as soon as December 7th.

Alen was doing his last bit of yard work on the house when his phone rang. His rumbling stomach told him it was lunch time. He reached into his pocket for his phone, and as he expected, it was Joan calling.

Hi! I found us a house sit! From December 13th until January 3rd."

"Really? That's great. Where are we going?

"Edinburgh!"

"Scotland?"

"Yeah, Scotland. And I'm buying you a kilt for Christmas! And guess what else?"

"I'm hung up on kilt, but what else?

"We'll be sitting with a border collie named Sherlock!"

"That's great, Sweetheart! This is going to be the best Christmas ever. But wait...I hope a dog named Sherlock doesn't portend what's waiting for us in Scotland."

"Oh, Alen, don't be silly."

The End

The next book in the House Sitters Cozy Mystery Series: **Exposed in Edinburgh!**

Get it now: books2read.com/u/4Ex5Rz

Turn the page for A message from Scarlett, Info about Exposed in Edinburgh, Joan's Texas Caviar and Velvety Chocolate Butter Pecan Pie recipes, pictures from Corpus Christi, and About the Author.

A message from Scarlett:

Hello, I know you have over a million choices of books to read. I can't tell you how much it means to me that you chose to spend some of your limited and valued reading time reading one of my books.

I truly appreciate it and hope I entertained you. If I did, I would appreciate a few more minutes of your time, if I may humbly ask, for you to leave a review for other readers who might be trying to select their next reading material.

If for any reason you were not satisfied with this book, let me know how I can do better by emailing me directly at
scarlett.moss@scarlettbraden.com.

The satisfaction of my readers and your feedback is important to me.

Hugs from Ecuador,
Scarlett

The next book in the House Sitters Cozy Mystery Series is...

Exposed in Edinburgh

Can a retired sheriff with shattered confidence ever trust his gut instincts again?

Expectations of castles, kilts, and bagpipes turn into undercover crime solving where even the English language is a mystery.

Alen and Joan Arny happily left law enforcement behind in exchange for traveling and new adventures. They never expected their new job as house and pet sitters to lead them back to crime and intrigue.

Ian Bennett has a secret. He's in big trouble if it's exposed and someone is threatening to do just that. The American couple house sitting next door might be the answer to his prayers.

Alen and Joan question if it's possible to solve a mystery and capture a criminal with no police department, authority, jurisdiction, crime scene analysis, forensics, or modern crime solving technology.

Will Alen be able to trust his intuition through his self-doubt, will Joan consider crime solving a bucket list worthy adventure, and can a canine named Sherlock Holmes help at all?

Read it today, because we love a cozy mystery where the good guys prevail and dogs help save the day.

Exposed in Edinburgh is the first book in the series.

A clean cozy mystery. No graphic violence, sex, or strong language. Available in Large Print.

The House Sitters Cozy Mysteries will take you on adventures and land you in the middle of crimes in different international cities in each book. Enjoy travel photos and recipes from each destination along with charming dogs in each country. Each book can be read as a standalone and you can read them in any order.

Get **Exposed in Edinburgh** today

books2read.com/u/4Ex5Rz

Joan's Texas Caviar

Ingredients

2 cans (15-1/2 ounces each) black-eyed peas, rinsed and drained

1 can (10 ounces) diced tomatoes and green chilies, drained

1 medium green pepper, finely chopped

1 small red onion, finely chopped

1/2 cup fat-free Italian salad dressing

2 tablespoons lime juice

1/4 teaspoon salt

1/4 teaspoon pepper

1 medium ripe avocado, peeled and cubed

Tortilla chips

Directions

In a large bowl, combine the peas, tomatoes, green pepper and onion. In a small bowl, whisk the dressing, lime juice, salt and pepper. Pour over black-eyed pea mixture and stir to coat. Cover and refrigerate for at least 1 hour.

Stir in avocado just before serving. Serve with chips.

Joan's Velvety Chocolate

Butter Pecan Pie

Ingredients

1-1/4 cups all-purpose flour

1 tablespoon sugar

1/2 teaspoon salt

1/3 cup cold butter

2 tablespoons butter-flavored shortening

3 to 4 tablespoons ice water

1/2 teaspoon white vinegar

1/4 teaspoon vanilla extract

EGG WASH:

1 large egg

1 tablespoon water

FILLING:

1/2 cup butter

4 ounces bittersweet chocolate, chopped

1-1/4 cups packed brown sugar

3/4 cup light corn syrup

3 large eggs, lightly beaten

2 tablespoons molasses

1 teaspoon vanilla extract

1/2 teaspoon salt

1-1/2 cups finely chopped pecans

1/2 cup pecan halves

Directions

In a large bowl, combine the flour, sugar and salt; cut in the butter and shortening until crumbly. Combine water, vinegar and vanilla. Gradually add to flour mixture, tossing with a fork until dough forms a ball. Wrap in plastic; refrigerate for 8 hours or overnight.

Roll out pastry to fit a 9-in. pie plate. Transfer pastry to pie plate. Trim pastry to 1/2 in. beyond edge of plate; flute edges. Beat egg wash ingredients; brush over pastry.

For filling, melt butter and chocolate in a microwave; stir until smooth. In a large bowl, combine the brown sugar, corn syrup, eggs, molasses, vanilla and salt. Stir in chopped pecans and butter mixture. Pour into pastry. Arrange pecan halves over filling.

Bake at 350° for 55-65 minutes or until a knife inserted in the center comes out clean. Cover edges with foil during the last 15 minutes to prevent overbrowning if necessary. Cool on a wire rack. Refrigerate leftovers.

Corpus Christi Photos

Corpus Christi Church was formerly a synagogue. Picture by eestellez

Wind Dancer Sculpture in Cole Park, Corpus Christi, Texas Photo by damoney777.

Dog and Feet Sculpture at American Bank Center in Corpus Christi photo by Gail Rubin

A pelican in Corpus Christi photo by awsloley

If you have travel photos you would like to submit for future books, please email ScarlettBraden@gmail.com.

About the Author

Scarlett Moss is a pen name for Scarlett Braden's cozy mystery books. Scarlett also writes thrillers and poetry.

Originally from the southern United States, Scarlett now calls the Andes mountains of Ecuador home. She lives there with her husband and her Ecuadorian pound puppy, Picasso.

Scarlett found her writing voice and her passion for writing late in life and now it's her favorite thing to do, usually with Picasso, the writer's assistant, by her side or in her lap. She also enjoys the festivals and holidays of her adopted country.

If you would like to hang out with Scarlett, she would love to have you in her Facebook readers group called Scarlett's Safe Room: Straight Jackets Optional where you can get to know her better, enjoy her twisted sense of humor, and sometimes even win prizes. You can join here:

https://www.facebook.com/groups/ScarlettsSafeRoom/

If you just want to lurk and follow the progress of her cozy mystery books, you can follow the Scarlett Moss Facebook page here: https://www.facebook.com/ScarlettMossMysteries

Sign up for the cozy mystery newsletter to be informed when new books are released or sales are going on here:

http://eepurl.com/gMu0G1

Made in the USA
Las Vegas, NV
11 February 2021

17649203R00069